1 3 5 7 9 10 8 6 4 2

Vintage
20 Vauxhall Bridge Road,
London SW1V 2SA

Vintage Classics is part of the Penguin Random House
group of companies whose addresses can be found at
global.penguinrandomhouse.com

Penguin
Random House
UK

Birdsong first published in Great Britain by Hutchinson in 1993
Where My Heart Used to Beat first published in Great Britain by Hutchinson
in 2015
A Week in December first published in Great Britain by Hutchinson in 2009
This edition published by Vintage in 2018

penguin.co.uk/vintage

A CIP catalogue record for this book is available from the British Library

ISBN 9781784874490

Typeset in 9.5/14.5 pt FreightText Pro
by Jouve (UK), Milton Keynes
Printed and bound by Clays Ltd, St Ives plc

Penguin Random House is committed to a sustainable future for
our business, our readers and our planet. This book is made from
Forest Stewardship Council® certified paper.

FSC
www.fsc.org
MIX
Paper from
responsible sources
FSC® C018179

War

SEBASTIAN FAULKS

VINTAGE MINIS

Birdsong

JACK FIREBRACE LAY forty-five feet underground with several hundred thousand tons of France above his face. He could hear the wooden wheezing of the feed that pumped air through the tunnel. Most of it was exhausted by the time it reached him. His back was supported by a wooden cross, his feet against the clay, facing towards the enemy. With an adapted spade, he loosened quantities of soil into a bag which he passed back to Evans, his mate, who then crawled away in the darkness. Jack could hear the hammering of timbers being used to shore up the tunnel further back, though where he worked, at the face, there was no guarantee that the clay would hold.

The sweat ran down into his eyes and stung them, making him shake his head from side to side. At this point the tunnel was about four feet across and five feet high. Jack kept sticking the spade into the earth ahead of him, hacking it out as though he hated it. He had lost track of how long he had been underground. He found it easier not to think when he might be relieved, but to keep digging. The harder he worked, the easier it seemed. It must have been six hours or more since he had seen daylight, and even then not much of it, but a thin green haze across the lowlands of the French–Belgian border, lit by the spasmodic explosion of shells.

His unit had not been able to return to its billet in the local village. So intense was the activity in this part of the line that the surface troops would not stay in their trenches without the protection of the men underground. The miners had to sleep, for the time being, in chambers at the top of their shafts or in the trenches with the infantry.

Jack felt a hand clutch his elbow. 'Jack. We need you. Turner's heard something about twenty yards back. Come on.'

Evans pulled him off the cross, and Jack turned stiffly, easing the sweat-soaked vest off his shoulders, and following Evans's crawling buttocks until he could stand. Even the murk of the timbered tunnel was bright to him after the clay face. He blinked in the gloom.

'Over here, Firebrace. Turner said it sounded like digging.'

Captain Weir, a startling figure with disarrayed hair, in plimsolls and civilian sweater, pushed him over to where Turner, a tired, frightened man, shivering with fatigue in the hot tunnel, was resting against his pick.

'It was just here,' said Turner. 'I'd got my head close up to this timber and I could hear vibrations. It wasn't our lot, I can tell you.'

Jack placed his head against the wall of the tunnel. He could hear the rhythmic gasp of the bellows in the overhead hosepipe draped from the ceiling. 'You'll have to turn off the air-feed, sir,' he said to Weir.

'Christ,' said Turner, 'I can't breathe.'

Weir dispatched a message to the surface. Two minutes later the noise ceased and Jack knelt down again. His exceptional hearing was frequently in demand. The previous winter, two miles south of Ypres, he had lowered his ear to rat-level in the trench into a water-filled petrol can and held it there until his head lost all feeling. He preferred the airless quiet of the tunnel to the numbing of his skull.

The men stood motionless as Weir held his finger to his lips. Jack breathed in deeply and listened, his body rigid with effort. There were sounds, distant and irregular. He could not be sure what they were. If they evacuated the tunnel as a precaution and the noise turned out only to have been shellfire or surface movement then time would be lost on their own tunnel. On the other hand, if he failed to identify German digging coming back the other way, the loss of life would probably be greater. He had to be sure.

'For God's sake, Firebrace.' He heard Weir's hissing voice in his ear. 'The men can hardly breathe.'

Jack held up his hand. He was listening for the distinctive knocking made by timber when it was hammered into place against the wall. If a tunnel was very close it was also sometimes possible to hear the sound of spades or of bags of earth being dragged back.

There was a thumping noise again, but it did not sound hollow enough for wood; it was more like the rocking of the earth under shellfire. Jack tightened his nerves once more. His concentration was interrupted by a noise like the delivery of a sack of potatoes. Turner had collapsed on to the tunnel floor. Jack made up his mind.

He said, 'Shellfire.'

'Are you sure?' said Weir.

'Yes, sir. As sure as I can be.'

'All right. Tell them to turn the air-feed on again. Firebrace, you get back on the cross. You two, get Turner on his feet.'

Jack crawled back into the darkness, feet first, where Evans helped him regain his position and passed him the spade. He sank it into the earth ahead of him, feeling glad of the resumption of mechanical toil. Evans's grubbing hands worked invisibly beside him. Towards the end of his shift he began to imagine things. He thought for a second that he was standing in the lighted bar of a London pub, holding up his beer glass to the lamp, looking at the big gilt mirror behind the bar. The bright reflection made him blink, and the flickering of his eyes brought back the reality of the clay wall ahead of him. Evans's hand scraped. Jack struck out ahead of him again, his arms grinding in their joints.

Evans swore beneath his breath and Jack reached out and gripped him in rebuke. Evans had tried to light a candle but there was not enough oxygen. The match burned bright red but would not flame. The two men stopped and listened. They could hear the roar of their breathing magnified in the silence. They held their breath and there was nothing. They had dug to the end of the world. Jack could smell the damp earth and the sweat from Evans's body. Normally he could hear the timbers behind them being put into place by hand, pushed quietly against the clay. There was not even this cautious sound. The narrow tunnel closed round them. Jack felt Evans's hand grip his arm. His breath rasped out again. Something must be happening behind them.

'All right,' Jack said. 'Get me off this thing.'

Evans pulled the wooden support away and helped roll Jack over. They crawled back until they saw lamplight. Weir was half-standing in the low tunnel. He clutched his ear, then gestured them to lean against the side walls. He began to mouth an explanation but before he could finish there was a roar in the tunnel and a huge ball of earth and rock blew past them. It took four men with it, their heads and limbs blown away and mixed with the rushing soil. Jack, Weir and Evans were flattened against the side wall by the blast and escaped the path of the debris. Jack saw part of Turner's face and hair still attached to a piece of skull rolling to a halt where the tunnel narrowed into the section he had been digging. There was an arm with a corporal's stripe on it near his feet, but most of the men's bodies had been blown into the moist earth.

Weir said, 'Get out before another one goes.'

Back towards the trench someone had already got a fresh lamp down into the darkness.

Jack took Evans's shoulder. 'Come on, boy. Come on now.'

It was dusk on the surface and the rain was falling. Stretcher-bearers pushed past Jack as he stood blinking at the top of the tunnel, breathing the damp air. Weir dismissed the men and went to find a field telephone. Jack walked from the tunnel head to his place in the trench.

'Letter for you, Jack,' said Bill Tyson. 'Mail came this morning.'

They sat huddled beneath a wooden frame with a groundsheet stretched over it. Arthur Shaw, the third man who shared their shelter, was trying to make tea on a primus stove.

Jack's letter was from his wife in Edmonton. 'My Dearest Jack,' it started. 'How are you keeping?'

He folded it away inside his pocket. He could not bring his mind to bear on the distant world her handwriting suggested. He was afraid he would not understand her letter, that she would be telling him something important his mind was too tired to register. He drank the tea Shaw had conjured from the gloom.

'Turner's dead,' he said. 'And at least two others.'

'Didn't you hear anything?' said Tyson.

'Yes, but I thought it was shellfire. There must be a tunnel.'

'Don't worry,' said Tyson. 'Anyone can make a mistake.'

There was a whining sound in the air about a hundred yards to their right as another shell came over.

'Any news about when we're getting out of here?' said Jack.

'Supposed to be tomorrow,' said Shaw, 'but I can't see us getting down the line while this shelling's going on. Did Weir say anything?'

'No, I don't think he knows.'

The three men looked at each other with expressionless, exhausted eyes. Tyson and Shaw had been together for a year, since they had been drawn to enlist by the six shillings pay on offer to men with experience of working underground. Both had been miners in Nottingham, though Tyson had done little work beneath the surface, having been chiefly concerned with the maintenance of machinery. Shaw claimed to be thirty-one, but might have been ten years older. He would work like a packhorse in the tunnel but had little enthusiasm for the military discipline imposed on them by the infantry.

In Jack's life they had replaced two fellow-Londoners with whom he had worked on the construction of the Central Line. Both these men, Allen and Mortimer, had died in an explosion on the Messines Ridge near Ypres the year before. Jack, already immune to death, let their white faces drift from his memory. He had succumbed only with reluctance to the friendship of Tyson and Shaw, but found to his dismay that their company had grown important to him. When they lay down to sleep, he let Shaw rest his head on his knees, which were folded inwards to keep out of the line of the trench itself. Sometimes he awoke to find a rat had crawled across his face. At other hours he lay rocked between the fear of being buried by a shell, consumed in the earth they had crawled under, and the overpowering need to lose consciousness of the noise that assailed them. There were wooden planks beneath them which seemed to lie against their bones. Even Shaw's big flanks and shoulders gave him no cushioning of flesh as he rolled and tossed in half-sleep.

Captain Weir's face appeared round the corner of the groundsheet. He was wearing a waterproof cape over his white sweater and had changed into knee-length rubber boots.

'Shaw, you're needed in the tunnel,' he said. 'I know you were in this morning, but they need help to clear the debris. You'd better report for duty, too, Tyson.'

'I'm on sentry duty at ten, sir.'

'Firebrace will have to do it for you. Come on, move yourselves. Sergeant Adams is in charge of the working party. Go and report to him.'

'Finish my tea, Jack,' said Shaw. 'Don't let the rats have it.'

With the others gone, Jack tried to sleep. His nerves were too stretched. He closed his eyes but could see only the dark of the tunnel face. He kept hearing the sudden quiet that had made him and Evans stop and hold their breath. He did not berate himself for failing to identify the sound of a German tunnel. He had done his best, and the men might have died anyway, perhaps in a worse way, with gas in their lungs or lying beyond help in no man's land. They would find that part of Turner's face and head and they would bury it beneath the earth with any other bits of bone and uniform they could bring back from underground. He thought of Shaw's big hands sifting through the blown soil. For a moment he relaxed into sleep, but then the decontraction of his body made him jump and he awoke again, his body tensed and ready to fight.

Abandoning sleep, he took out the letter from his breast pocket and lit a stub of candle he found in the side compartment of Tyson's pack.

> My Dearest Jack, How are you keeping? All our thoughts and prayers are with you. We read the newspapers each day, we look at the casualty columns first. There doesn't seem to be any news of where you are. We have had Mother staying and she says to tell you she got your letter and she is sending another parcel with some soap and cigarettes and some gooseberries from the garden. I hope they won't be too ripe by the time they get to you.
>
> I am very sorry to have to tell you little John has been taken ill. He has been very poorly indeed and the doctor says it is diphtheria. He was in hospital in Tottenham last week and he is a little better, but his temperature is still very high. As you will imagine it is not easy getting

medicine and the doctors to look after him with so much going to the men at the front which is how it should be.

He is in good spirits when he is awake and we have seen him in the hospital. He asks me to send you his love. I am sorry to bother you with this news but I think it is for the best. He does miss you very much and I know he loves you. Our prayers are with you and I send my love to you, From Margaret.

With the mail had come rations. There were some tins of stew and bully beef which were held over to midday, but there was bread and jam to go with half a mug of tea. Hungry from his work underground, Jack ate quickly at an improvised station at the head of the communication trench. Sometimes the men who brought the rations had unreliable news of troop movements and plans from behind the lines; today there was no word. Jack ate in silence before returning to his position.

His son John had been born eight years before, when Margaret was nearly forty and they had almost despaired of having children. He was a bright-eyed boy, thin and fair, with a vacant expression that often gave way to shrill laughter. His physical frailty was compounded by the simplicity of his mind. He was tolerated by the other boys in the street when they needed someone to make up numbers. He was the goalkeeper in their unrefereed games of football and was allowed to bat at cricket only in an emergency.

Jack looked closely at his wife's careful handwriting and tried to bring the boy's face to mind. In the murk of the rainy evening, with only Tyson's piece of candle for light, it was difficult to see. He closed his eyes and pictured his son's knees beneath the ragged grey shorts, the big teeth he revealed when he smiled, the untidy hair through which he would sometimes run a fatherly hand.

At the front he hardly ever thought of home. In his wallet was a picture of Margaret, but none of John. There was always too much to think of to allow his mind to dwell on inessentials. He had not been home for almost a year. He found it unbelievable when Shaw told him that if the atmospheric conditions were right the guns could be heard in London. The place in which he often found himself, often underground, with no clear idea of where the nearest village was, seemed as distant from those streets and houses as if he now inhabited another world.

That night he stood on the firestep at the end of the trench on sentry duty for Tyson, who had still not returned from underground. The miners were not supposed to do sentry duty, but their officer had struck a deal with his opposite number in the infantry. In view of enemy activity and the consequent danger underground, the infantry would provide fighting cover in the tunnels in return for the miners doing some of their fatigues. For Jack the days and nights had ceased to be distinct. There was the darkness of the tunnel, the twilight of late afternoon under the intermittent light of shellfire and the blackness of the trench at night beneath the curtain of a groundsheet.

He listened for noises from the no-man's-land in front of him. German night patrols had been out, with the aim of checking on enemy movements and spreading anxiety. Jack imagined that his side, too, had men in listening posts who would hear anything before he did, but in his trench the sentries were never told in case it made them complacent. The infantry battalion came from London; they referred to the tunnellers as 'sewer rats' and were anxious to prove how ineffective they were as soldiers.

Jack was so tired that he had passed the stage when sleep was possible. His body had found some automatic course, powered by what source of wakefulness he couldn't say, that kept him awake if not alert while other men nodded and dozed on the ground, some slumped as though dead on the floor of the trench, some leaning with their backs to the wooden boards. From further down the line he could hear trench repair parties at work.

John's face was now in his mind quite brightly: the wan, solitary boy at the tail of the street gang, the stumbling baby with his troublesome steps. He could hear his piping London voice with its parrot greetings and unfounded optimism. He pictured his boy in the high-ceilinged hospital ward with the yellow smudge of gas lamps, the starched headdresses of the nurses and the smell of soap and disinfectant.

Sleep came to him like an unseen assailant. It was not

the sinister light of the ward but the lamps of a huge bar in a pub on Lea Bridge Road: the men in suits and flat caps, smoke rising, ale glasses held aloft. There were other pictures, end to end: the kitchen of his parents' house in Stepney; a park, a dog; the lit pub again, thronged with people; John's face, the dear boy. He was aware of a great temptation being offered, some ease of mind, some sleep for which he would sell the lives of his comrades, and he embraced the offer, not aware that he was already slumbering, head slumped forwards, cradled between the aching shoulders that had dug out French earth for hours without respite.

He did not know he was asleep until he was awake again, feeling himself slump forwards as a boot cracked into his ankle.

'What's your name?' It was an officer's voice.

'Firebrace, sir.'

'Oh, it's you, Firebrace.' He recognised Captain Weir's surprised tone.

'Were you asleep?' The first officer's voice was cold.

'I don't know, sir. I just wasn't listening and –'

'You were asleep on duty. It's a court-martial offence. See me tomorrow at six. Your sergeant will bring you. You know the punishment.'

'Yes, sir.'

Jack watched the two men walk on and swing left at the end of the firebay, the red ends of their cigarettes glowing.

He was relieved by Bob Wheeler, another tunneller. He went back to find Tyson and Shaw asleep beneath their wooden frame. There was no room for him with them, so he took a handful of cigarettes from his pack and went back down the communication trench, past the half-hearted challenge of a sentry. He climbed over the back of the support trench and found himself in an area where piles of ammunition and supplies lay strapped under tarpaulin in the drizzle. There was a group of men, including a sergeant, on guard near by and he went to make himself known to them. He told them he was going to the latrines, and they let him pass.

He found a tree that had not been damaged by shellfire and sat down beneath it, lighting a cigarette and sucking in the smoke. Before the war he had never touched tobacco; now it was his greatest comfort.

If he was found guilty by court martial he could be shot. The tunnellers had become more and more part of the army; although they had not undergone the humiliating drills and punishments handed out to the infantry before they were deemed ready to fight, they had lost the separate status they had had at first. When Jack had arrived at Ypres with his fellow-Londoners Allen and Mortimer, he was told they would spend the war there while different divisions of infantry came and went, but to begin with they found themselves in a constant and bewildering state of movement, the very trouble the organisation had been designed to prevent. They had become soldiers and were expected to kill the enemy not only by mining but with bayonet or bare hands if necessary.

This was not the life Jack had envisaged when he volunteered. At the age of thirty-eight he could reasonably have avoided service, but he had no work in London. Margaret was ten years older than him and had enough to do looking after John. She managed cleaning jobs from time to time, but the money was not enough for them. Jack didn't think the war would last long; he told Margaret he would be home within the year, having saved half his pay.

She was a practical woman of Irish descent who was drawn to Jack by his humour and his kindliness. They had met at the wedding of one of her eight sisters, who was marrying a workmate of Jack's. At the party after the service Jack was drinking beer and doing conjuring tricks for a group of children. He had a big, square face with hair parted in the middle. She liked the way he talked to the children before he began joking with the other men who had come along to see their friend married.

'I'm an old maid,' she told Jack when he went round to visit her a week later. 'You don't want to be walking out with me.' But he seemed to know exactly what he wanted and they were married three months later.

Lighting another cigarette beneath his tree, listening to the screech of a shell going over the British line about half a mile south, Jack Firebrace began to tremble.

He had thought himself immune to death; he thought he had hardened himself against it, but it was not so. If they found him guilty they would take him alone at daybreak to some secluded place behind the lines – a glade in a forest, a yard behind a farm wall – and shoot him dead. They would ask members of his own unit, miners and diggers, men who had not even been trained to fire on the enemy, to do the job. Some would have blanks and some would not; no one would know whether the fatal shot had been fired by Tyson or Shaw or Wheeler or Jones. He would fall like the millions of the dead who had gone down into the mud: baker's boys from Saxony, farm labourers from France and factory workers from Lancashire, so much muscle and blood in the earth.

He could not look on this possibility without shaking. When there was a battle or a raid, they expected to die; it was the losses through sniper fire, through shells and mortars, the blowing of the tunnel, the continuous awareness that any moment could bring death in a number of different ways that had been harder to understand. Slowly Jack had become accustomed even to this. It took him a day of sleep each time they went in to rest before he could adjust to not being in constant fear; then he would begin to laugh and tell stories in the surging relief that overcame them. The indifference he had cultivated, however, was to the extermination of the enemy, his colleagues and his friends; he was not, he now admitted to himself, indifferent to the prospect of his own death.

He held his face in his hands and prayed to God to save him. There was no task he wanted to complete, no destiny

He would fall like the millions of the dead who had gone down into the mud: baker's boys from Saxony, farm labourers from France and factory workers from Lancashire, so much muscle and blood in the earth.

by which he felt impelled: he merely wanted to see Margaret again. He wanted to touch John's hair. My son, he thought, as he sat in the rain, my darling boy. It would make no difference to the outcome of the war whether he himself lived or died; it made no difference whether today it was Turner whose head was blown from his body, or whether tomorrow it was his or Shaw's or Tyson's. Let them die, he prayed, shamefully; let them die, but please God let me live.

Through the night he sat unchallenged and alone, forcing his exhausted mind to bring out memories of his life, pictures of what he had done that might go with him and comfort him if he had to face the line of rifles pointed at his heart. There were games of football on Hackney Marshes, the comradeship of workers on the construction of the London Underground; odd faces and voices from childhood; his son. There was nothing to make it seem a life worth saving. In the end his memory offered him only fragments of early childhood: sitting in front of the kitchen range, the smell of his mother as she kissed him in his bed. With them came a desire to sleep, to surrender.

He stood up and stretched his stiff arms and legs, then slunk back to his position in the trench and crept in beside Tyson and Shaw. Shortly before dawn he went to look for Sergeant Adams.

'Come along, then,' said Adams. 'Smarten yourself. Get your belt on straight.'

He was not the kind of sergeant most men feared. He had a mocking sense of humour and seldom shouted. The men privately admired him.

'I've heard all about you, sleeping on the job,' he said.

Jack said nothing. He was ready to die.

'You may be lucky. Some of these young officers blow hot and cold. Mr Wraysford is the strangest one I've seen. Law unto himself. This way.'

Adams walked him down a narrow trench in the rear of which were several dugouts. He pointed to an entrance at the end of the line and told him to go down on his own.

Jack looked up at the rim of the world that was appearing through the grey light: the burned and blasted trees, the once-green fields now uniformly brown where all the earth had been turned by shells. He was reconciled to leaving it.

He went down the wooden ladder and found a gas curtain across a home-made door. He knocked and waited.

A voice told him to come in and he wrenched the door open. There was a strong smell of paraffin inside. Pipe smoke obscured the contents of the room. Jack was able to make out a wooden bunk in the lower half of which a figure lay hunched in sleep, and a makeshift table and chairs. It was better made than most of the squalid arrangements he had seen, though the primitive boarding that made the walls and the tinker's use of odd cups, candles, wicks and nails to do duty for missing essentials gave it a primitive appearance.

'Who are you?' He was addressed by a lieutenant, who was one of two officers sitting at the table. The other was Jack's own company commander, Captain Weir, on a visit to the infantry.

'Firebrace, sir. You told me to report to you at six this morning.'

'Why?'

'I was asleep on sentry duty.'

The officer stood up and walked over to where Jack was standing. He brought his face up close. Jack saw a man with dark hair that was going grey at the sides; he had a thick moustache that obscured his upper lip and big brown eyes that stared thoughtfully at him. He might have been any age from twenty-five to forty.

'I have no recollection at all.'

'I think you were going to put me on a charge, sir.'

'I don't think I could do that. You're not in my unit. You're a tunneller, aren't you?'

'Yes, sir.'

'One of yours, Weir.'

Jack looked towards Weir and noticed the almost empty bottle of whisky that stood on the table. There were only two glasses.

'Sit down, Firebrace. Have a drink,' said Weir.

'No thank you, sir. If I –'

'Sit down anyway.'

Jack looked round. He didn't want to sit on a chair that might belong to the officer commanding the infantry, an irascible man called Gray whom he had heard giving orders. He wondered where he was: bullying the sentries, perhaps.

Jack took the chair that Weir kicked towards him. Weir was back in his soft shoes and white sweater. He looked unshaven and his eyes were bloodshot. Jack looked down, afraid to meet his gaze. Also on the table were five playing cards laid out in the shape of a star, face down, with thin trails of sand between them. In the centre of the formation was a carved wooden figure and a stump of candle.

'This is Lieutenant Wraysford,' said Weir. 'His platoon is next to your section in the line. His are the men we are protecting against mines. Last night he had two men out in a listening post. Perhaps he was worried about them. Is that right, Wraysford?'

'No. Brennan and Douglas would be all right. They know what they're doing.'

'Don't you want to talk to this man?' said Weir.

'I would if I could remember who he was.' He turned to Jack. 'There'll be some tea in a minute if you don't want whisky. I'll tell Riley to make an extra cup.'

As Jack's eyes grew accustomed to the smoky dugout he saw that parts of the walls were covered with fabric. It looked like expensive foreign silk or cotton. On top of a small locker were more wooden carvings of human figures. There were no photographs on the bookshelves in the corner, though there were some amateurish sketches of heads and bodies. He became aware that the lieutenant had been following his gaze.

'Do you draw?'

'A bit,' said Jack. 'I don't get enough time now. Or the quiet.'

A tray with three mugs of tea was brought in by Riley, a small grey-haired man in neat uniform. He reached up to a bag suspended from the ceiling, out of range of rats, and produced some sugar.

Jack watched the lieutenant go over to the shelves and take down a sketch. 'The human anatomy is extraordinarily simple,' he said. 'The construction of the legs for instance: two long bones with a simple joint for flexing, and the proportions always the same. But when you draw them it's difficult to suggest the shape. Everyone can see this muscle on the thigh, the quadriceps. I never knew there was another one here, inside, the sartorius. But if you emphasise it too much the figure looks muscle-bound.'

Jack watched the lieutenant's finger trace the lines of the leg on the drawing as he spoke. He was not sure whether the man was teasing him, extending his agony, or whether he really wanted to talk about drawing.

'Of course,' the lieutenant said with a sigh, 'the war has provided all of us with daily lessons in anatomy. I could write a paper on the major organs of the British private soldier. Liver in section. Bowel, extent of, when eviscerated. The powdery bone of the average English subaltern.'

Jack coughed. 'Excuse me, sir. Can I ask about the charge?'

'The charge?'

'For God's sake, Wraysford,' said Weir. 'You told this man to report to you because he was asleep. He wants to know if you are going to have him court-martialled. He wants to know if he's going to have an art lesson or whether he's going to be shot.'

'There's no charge. You are not under my command.'

Jack felt a hot stinging in his eyes.

'I'm sure your own company commander will punish you if he wants to.'

Weir shook his head. 'No further action.'

'Thank you, sir. Thank you.'

Jack looked at the two men with love and gratitude. They understood the difficulties of a man who had been stretched too far. He felt sure that their mercy sprang from compassion for him. He took out Margaret's letter. In his enthusiasm for living he wanted to share the burden of his son's illness.

'You see here, sir. I had this letter from my wife. Our boy's been taken poorly. I was worried about him. I'd not slept when I came up from the tunnel, I was so worried about him.'

He handed the letter to Weir, who nodded. 'See this, Wraysford?' he said, pushing it across the table.

'Yes,' said Stephen. 'I see it. Diphtheria, it says. That's serious.'

'Will I be allowed leave to go and see him?'

Stephen raised an eyebrow towards Weir. 'I doubt it. We're undermanned as it is,' said Weir.

Jack said, 'Have you got children, sir?'

Weir shook his head. 'Not married.'

'You, sir?'

'No,' said Stephen.

Jack nodded a few times to himself. 'I suppose it's funny when I'm out here with men getting killed all round me and it's him that's in danger.'

Stephen said, 'Every one of the men we've killed is someone's son. Do you think of that when you see them dead? Do you wonder what their mothers thought when they first held them to their breast – that they would end like this?'

'No, sir. I hadn't thought of it like that.'

The three men drank their tea. From the outside came the whining of shells. They could feel the reverberation of the explosions in the dugout. Fragments of dried earth fell from the ceiling.

Stephen said, 'Two of my men were in a shellhole listening for eight hours last night in no man's land. What do you think they were thinking about all that time? It's not as if they're allowed to talk.' He was looking at Jack.

'I don't know, sir. Perhaps it's like when we're in the tunnel. You stop thinking at all after a bit. It's as though you've stopped living. Your mind goes dead.'

'I'd like to go down your tunnel,' said Stephen.

'No you wouldn't,' said Weir. 'Even the miners don't like it.'

'I'd like to see what it feels like. Some of my men think you don't work fast enough down there. They think you don't hear the noise of the enemy. They're terrified of being blown up from underneath.'

Weir laughed. 'We know that all right.'

Jack shifted in his chair. There was something strange about the two officers. He suspected they were drunk. He had always thought of Weir as dependable. Like all the tunnelling company commanders, he was a Regular Engineer who had been transferred. He was careful and reliable underground, even though he had had no experience of it before the war. But his eyes looked wild and red with whisky. The brownish stubble on his cheeks and chin was surely the result of more than one morning's missed shave. The lieutenant, Jack thought, looked more sober, but in some ways even stranger. You could not be sure whether he was serious. He seemed forgetful and distant, but also enthusiastic about going underground. It was as though he was not all there, Jack thought. The affection and gratitude he had felt at first began to evaporate. He didn't want to share any more of his personal feelings with them. He wanted to be back with Tyson and Shaw, or even Wheeler and Jones with their irritating chatter. At least with them he would know where he was.

'Any idea when we'll get some rest, sir?' he asked Weir.

'Tomorrow, I should think. They couldn't keep us here longer than that. What about your men, Wraysford?'

Stephen sighed. 'God knows. I hear rumours all the time from battalion headquarters. We will have to attack sooner or later. Not here though.'

'Are we going to have to lose a few lives just to placate the French?' Weir laughed.

'Yes. Oh, yes. They want to feel they're not alone in this. But I believe they will reap the whirlwind.'

Riley appeared from the back of the dugout. 'It's nearly six, sir. Stand-to in ten minutes.'

'You'd better go, Firebrace,' said Weir.

'I'll see you in that tunnel,' said Stephen.

'Thank you, sir.'

Jack climbed back out of the dugout. It was almost light outside. The low sky of Flanders met the earth at a short horizon, only a few miles behind the German lines. He breathed in deeply on the morning air. His life had been spared; the last trace of elation came to him as he looked towards the back of the trench and saw the plumes from cigarettes and steam from the tea that cold hands were now clasping. He thought of the stench of his clothes, the lice along the seams, the men he was frightened to befriend in case their bodies came apart the next day in front of his eyes. It was the hour of Tyson's ablutions when he would empty his bowels into a paintpot and throw the contents over the top.

From the officers' dugout behind him came the sound

of piano music, a rising melody under the scratch of a thick gramophone needle.

. . .

STEPHEN'S SECTION OF the line had been shelled off and on for three days. They assumed a large attack was imminent. On the third morning he rose wearily in his dugout and pushed aside the gas curtain. His eyes felt heavy with fatigue. His body was running not on natural energy given by food and sleep but on some nervous chemical supplied by unknown glands. His mouth felt burned and sour all the way down to the gut. His skull was throbbing beneath the surface with a broken, accelerated pulse. A tremor was starting in his hand. He needed to go and reassure the men in his platoon.

He found Brennan and Douglas, two of the most experienced, sitting on the firestep white-faced, with perhaps sixty cigarette ends on the ground beside them.

Stephen exchanged pleasantries with them. He was not a popular officer. He found it difficult to think of words of encouragement or inspiration when he himself did not believe there was a purpose to the war or an end to it in sight. He had been reprimanded by the company commander, Captain Gray, a shrewd and forceful man, for telling one soldier he believed the war would grow very much worse before there was a chance of its getting better.

Brennan's comments on the shelling contained his usual quotient of obscenity. His favourite adjective appeared so often in his sentences that after a time Stephen had stopped noticing it. It was the same with all the men.

Stephen had been promoted from the ranks because he had a better education than most of the others and because those of the university subalterns who were not dead had taken on companies. Gray picked him out and sent him back to England for a spell with an officer cadet training unit. On his return to France he was given further instruction by staff officers in Béthune, though as far as he could see, the only decisive moment came during a game of football in which he was supposed to show his mettle. He obliged by fighting with a player on the other side and was taken on a hasty three-week tour of the front line by an asthmatic major who was making his first excursion from brigade headquarters. The major was insistent that Stephen should not see any of the men with whom he had joined up; he was to be re-presented to them as a different and superior being who had magically acquired the attributes of an officer. The major wheezed his farewells and Stephen found himself the possessor of a shiny belt, new boots and a deferential batman. He had not met any of his platoon before, though the men with whom he had trained and fought were only a hundred yards or so down the line.

'No word of when this will stop, then?' said Douglas.

'They never tell me. What do you think?'

'I wish they'd give it a break.'

'Just as well they stop for lunch.' It was the cheeriest thing Stephen could think of to say. 'You can't keep a German gunner from his sausage.' His dry mouth did not relish the forced jollity.

There was a tearing sound in the air as a gun was fired. It was a medium-sized piece whose shell made a clanking, rattling noise that at first sounded quaint, then suddenly alarming as it accelerated closer to them. Brennan and Douglas flattened themselves against the front of the trench as it went over. The ground shook and small pieces of earth rained down gently on their heads. Stephen saw that Douglas's hands were now shaking badly as he rubbed his face.

He nodded to the two men. 'It can't last for ever.'

Normally shelling was aimed at night towards the rear areas, at the guns and ammunition and stores. The pounding of the front line in daylight was usually the prelude to an attack, though Stephen suspected it could be a variation of tactics, or just inaccuracy.

He made his way along the trench and talked to other members of the platoon. They took their orders from the NCOs and regarded Stephen as little more than a symbol of some distant authority in front of whom they were supposed to behave well and be respectful. Because of his friendship with Weir, Stephen had learned almost as much about the tunnellers as about his own men. He realised when he spoke to them under the continuing shellfire that he was ignorant of their lives. They were mostly Londoners who had belonged to the Territorials before the war.

The ones he liked best were Reeves, Byrne and Wilkinson, a sardonic trio who, unlike Brennan and Douglas, never volunteered for anything dangerous but retained a compelling and relentless dislike for the enemy.

He found them together, as usual, though uncharacteristically silent. A battery of field guns had been increasing in activity over the last hour, Reeves reported. While he was talking they heard the spanking report of one being fired, followed by the screeching sound of the shell.

'We're getting those all the time now,' said Reeves. 'Listen.'

The three men lay close together. They feared shell wounds more than bullets because they had seen the damage they did. A direct hit would obliterate all physical evidence that a man had existed; a lesser one would rip pieces from him; even a contained wound brought greater damage to the tissue of the body than a bullet. Infection or gangrene often followed.

A sharp wailing began a few yards down the trench. It was a shrill, demented sound that cut through even the varying noises of gunfire. A youth called Tipper ran along the duck-boards, then stopped and lifted his face to the sky. He screamed again, a sound of primal fear that shook the others who heard it. His thin body was rigid and they could see the contortions of his facial muscles beneath the skin. He was screaming for his home.

Byrne and Wilkinson began swearing at him.

'Help me,' said Stephen to Reeves. He went and took the boy's arm and tried to sit him down on the firestep. Reeves gripped him from the other side. His eyes were fixed on the sky and neither Stephen nor Reeves was able to unlock the muscles of his neck and make him look downward.

Tipper's face appeared to have lost all its circulation. The whites of his eyes, only a few inches from Stephen's face, bore no red tracery of blood vessels; there was only a brown circle with a dilated pupil floating in an area of white which was enlarged by the spasmodic opening of the eye. The pupil seemed to grow blacker and wider, so that the iris lost all light and sense of life.

With no idea of where he was, the boy repeatedly and imploringly called out some private word that might have been a pet name for his father or mother. It was a noise of primitive fear. Stephen felt a sudden loosening of compassion, which he quelled as quickly as he could.

'Get him out,' he said to Reeves. 'I don't want this here. You and Wilkinson, get him to the MO.'

'Yes, sir.' Reeves and Wilkinson dragged the rigid body to the communication trench.

Stephen was shaken. This eruption of natural fear brought home how unnatural was the existence they were leading; they did not wish to be reminded of normality. By the time he returned to his dugout, he was angry. If the pretence began to break, then it would take lives with it.

There seemed to be no way in which they could confront this dread. At Ypres and in other actions they had been able to prepare themselves to die, but the shellfire unmanned them all again. Men who had prepared themselves to walk into machine guns or defend their trenches to the last could not face death in this shape. They pretended that it was more than this; it was the evidence of what they had seen. Reeves had searched for his brother but had found no trace to bury, not a lock of hair, not even a piece of boot. He told Stephen this with bitterness and disbelief. The shell that had taken him was of a size that had to be loaded by crane from a light railway; after flying six miles at altitude it had left a crater large enough to house a farm with outbuildings. It was no wonder, Reeves said, that there was no trace of his brother. 'I wouldn't mind,' he said, 'but he was my own flesh and blood.'

By the afternoon of the third day Stephen began to be worried about the effects on all the men in his platoon. He felt like a useless and unused link in the chain. The senior officers would not confide in him; the men took direction from the NCOs and comfort from themselves. The bombardment continued.

Stephen talked briefly to Harrington, the lieutenant who also shared Gray's dugout, then drank the tea Riley produced promptly at five. He went out to look at the late afternoon light. It had begun to rain again, but the shells kept coming along the blackened skyline, their flares like unexpected stars, in the grey-green, turbulent darkness.

Towards midnight Weir came to the dugout. He had run out of whisky and wanted some of Stephen's. He waited till Gray had gone out.

'How was your rest?' said Stephen.

'A long time ago,' said Weir, drinking deeply from the flask Stephen pushed over to him. 'We've been back for three days.'

'So you've been underground. It's the safest place to be.'

'The men come out of the hole in the ground and they find themselves under this. They don't know which is worse. It can't go on, can it? It just can't.'

'Take it easy, Weir. There's not going to be an attack. They're there to stay. Those big guns take almost a week to dig into their pits.'

'You're a cold bastard, aren't you, Wraysford? Just tell me something that'll make me stop shaking, that's all.'

Stephen lit a cigarette and put his feet up on the table. 'Do you want to listen to the shells or do you want to talk about something else?'

'It's that idiot Firebrace with his trained hearing. He's taught me how to distinguish between each gun. I can tell you the size of it, the path of the shell, where it's going, the likely damage.'

'But you liked the war when it started, didn't you?'

'What?' Weir sat up in his chair. He had a round, honest face with receding fair hair. What was left of it was generally standing on end, or uncombed after he had removed his cap. He was wearing a pyjama jacket and a white naval jersey. He settled back a little on his seat as he contemplated what Stephen had said. 'It seems impossible to believe now, but I suppose I did.'

'It's nothing to be ashamed of. We all had our reasons for joining up. Look at Price, our CSM. He's flourished here, hasn't he? What about you? Were you lonely?'

'I don't want to talk about England,' said Weir. 'I've got to think of staying alive. I've got eight men underground with a German tunnel coming at us the other way.'

'All right,' said Stephen. 'I'm going out to check on my men in half an hour anyway.'

The dugout shook with the reverberations of a huge shell. The lantern swung on the beam, the glasses jumped on the table, and bits of earth fell from the ceiling. Weir gripped Stephen's wrist.

'Talk to me, Wraysford,' he said. 'Talk to me about anything you like.'

'All right. I'll tell you something.' Stephen blew out a trail of cigarette smoke. 'I'm curious to see what's going to happen. There are your sewer rats in their holes three feet wide crawling underground. There are my men going mad under shells. We hear nothing from our commanding officer. I sit here, I talk to the men, I go on patrol and lie in the mud with machine guns grazing my neck. No one in

England knows what this is like. If they could see the way these men live they would not believe their eyes. This is not a war, this is an exploration of how far men can be degraded. I am deeply curious to see how much further it can be taken; I want to know. I believe that it has barely started. I believe that far worse things than we have seen will be authorised and will be carried out by millions of boys and men like my Tipper and your Firebrace. There is no depth to which they can't be driven. You see their faces when they go in to rest and you think they will take no more, that something in them will say, enough, no one can do this. But one day's sleep, hot food and wine in their bellies and they will do more. I think they will do ten times more before it's finished and I'm eager to know how much. If I didn't have that curiosity I would walk into enemy lines and let myself be killed. I would blow my own head off with one of these grenades.'

'You're mad,' said Weir. 'Don't you just want it to be over?'

'Yes, of course I do. But now that we have come this far I want to know what it means.'

Weir began to shake again as the sounds of the shells came closer. 'It's a mixed barrage. The field gun alternating with heavy artillery at intervals of –'

'Be quiet,' said Stephen. 'Don't torture yourself.'

Weir held his head in his hands. 'Talk to me about something, Wraysford. Talk to me about anything but this war. England, football, women, girls. Whatever you like.'

'Girls? What the men call their sweethearts?'

This is not a war, this is an exploration of how far men can be degraded.

'If you like.'

'I haven't thought about them for a long time. Constant shellfire is a cure for impure thoughts. I never think of women. They belong to a different existence.'

Weir was silent for a moment. Then he said, 'You know something? I've never ever been with a woman.'

'What? Never?' Stephen looked to see if he was serious. 'How old are you?'

'Thirty-two. I wanted to, I always wanted to, but it was difficult at home. My parents were very strict. One or two of the girls I asked out for the evening, well they . . . they always wanted to get married. Then there were the working girls in the town, but they would have just laughed at me.'

'Aren't you intrigued to know what it's like?'

'Yes, yes, of course. But now it's become such an issue, it's assumed such an importance in my life that it would be difficult.'

Stephen noticed that Weir had stopped listening to the shellfire. He was staring down at the glass in his hands, deep in concentration.

'Why don't you go to one of those places all the men go to in the villages? I'm sure you could find someone friendly, not too expensive.'

'You don't understand, Wraysford. It's not that easy. It's different for you. I suppose you've been with hundreds of women, have you?'

Stephen shook his head. 'Good God, no. There was a girl in my village who'd do it with anyone. All the boys lost their innocence with her. You had to give her a present – chocolate or money or something. She was a simple girl but we were all very grateful. She got pregnant of course, but no one knew who the father was. Some fifteen-year-old youth, probably.'

'Was that all?'

'No. There were some other girls. Boys expected to do it. They thought it was unhealthy to store it up. Even their mothers thought so. That's the difference between a Lincolnshire village and a town like – what was your home?'

'Leamington Spa.'

'Exactly! The price of respectability.' Stephen smiled. 'It was bad luck for you.'

'You're telling me.' Weir began to laugh.

'Well done.'

'What do you mean, "well done"?'

'You're laughing.'

'I'm drunk.'

'It doesn't matter.'

Weir poured another drink and tipped his chair back. 'So all those girls, Wraysford, tell me —'

'Not that many. Perhaps four or five. That was all.'

'However many. Tell me, was there one you loved? Was there one you did it with again and again?'

'Yes, I think there was.'

'Just one?'

'Yes, just one.'

'And what was that like? Was it different from the others?'

'Yes, I suppose it was. It was quite different. It became confused with other feelings.'

'You mean, you . . . you were in love with her, or what?'

'That's what you would call it. I didn't know at the time what it was. I was just aware of some compulsion. I couldn't stop it.'

'What happened to this woman?'

'She left.'

'Why?'

'I don't know. I went home one day and she hadn't even left a note or a message.'

'Were you married?'

'No.'

'What did you do?'

'Nothing. What could I do? I couldn't pursue her. I let her go.'

Weir was quiet for a moment. Then he said, 'But when you . . . you know, with her, was it a different feeling, a different experience from with the girl in the village? Or is it always the same?'

'By the time she left I don't think I was thinking about that. It felt more as though someone had died. As though you were a child and your mother or father had died. As though you were a child and your mother or father had vanished.' Stephen looked up. 'You must find out for yourself. Your next leave. Or maybe we can get you down the line somehow. One of my men will know.'

'Don't be ridiculous,' said Weir. 'Anyway, this woman. Do you think of her now? Do you have a keepsake?'

'I had a ring that belonged to her. I threw it away.'

'Don't you ever think of her when you're lying here at night hearing the guns outside?'

'No. Never.'

Weir shook his head. 'I don't understand. I'm sure I would.'

There was a momentary stillness outside. The two men looked at each other in the dim light, their faces grey and weary. Stephen envied the innocence still visible beneath the strain that showed in Weir's open features. He felt he had already lost all connection with any earthly happiness that might persist beyond the sound of guns. The scattered grey hairs at his temples and above his ears seemed to remind him that he was changed and could not return.

'So,' he said. 'Before the war. Were you lonely?'

'Yes, I was. I was still living with my parents, I didn't seem to be able to get away. The only thing I could think of was to join the army. My father knew someone in the Engineers, so that was it. I joined up in nineteen-twelve. You were right. I liked having a role. And I liked the comradeship. It was as simple as that. I had had no friends before, and suddenly I found that I had, if not the friendship then at least the company of hundreds of men of my age. When I was commissioned I found that some of them even looked up to me. It was a grand feeling.'

'You've done well,' said Stephen. 'They respect you.'

'No,' said Weir dismissively, 'they'd follow anyone who –'

'I mean it. You've done well with them.'

'Thank you, Wraysford.'

Stephen poured more whisky. He always hoped it would make him sleep, but in fact it made little difference. If sleep came it was as a gift and was as likely to come after tea as after alcohol.

'My men don't respect me,' he said. 'They respect Sergeant Price. They're frightened of him, anyway. And they do what the corporals tell them, Smith and Petrossian. But I'm irrelevant to them.'

'Nonsense,' said Weir. 'You're in there with them just as much as any other subaltern. You go on patrols. They must admire you.'

'But they don't respect me. And they're right not to. Do you know why? Because I don't respect them. Sometimes I think I despise them. What do they think they're doing, for God's sake?'

'You're a funny chap,' said Weir. 'I remember a major I met outside Ypres, in the Salient, who –'

The door to the dugout was pushed open. It was Hunt. 'You'd better come, sir,' he said to Stephen. 'Shell in our setion. There's a lot of casualties. Reeves, Wilkinson, I think.'

Stephen took his cap and followed Hunt out into the night.

The sandbags that made up the parapet had been blown away on a front of about twenty yards. The wall of the trench had caved in and barbed wire had been blown back and was hanging over the churned earth. There was a sound of groaning. Stretcher-bearers were trying to clear the debris to get to the wounded men. Stephen took a trenching tool and began to dig. They pulled out a man by his shoulders. It was Reeves. His expression was more vacant than usual. His ribcage was missing on one side where a large piece of shell casing stuck out from under his breastbone.

A few yards further on they disinterred Wilkinson. His dark profile looked promisingly composed as Stephen approached. He ran through his mind for Wilkinson's personal details. He remembered. He had just married. He worked as a bookmaker. There was a baby on the way. He prepared words of encouragement as he came alongside. But as the stretcher-bearers lifted him, they turned his body and Stephen saw that his head was cut away in section, so that the smooth skin and the handsome face remained on one side, but on the other were the ragged edges of skull from which the remains of his brain were dropping on to his scorched uniform.

He nodded to the stretcher-bearers. 'Take him away.'

Further on was another casualty, Douglas, whom he had seen that morning and thought indestructible. Douglas was alive and had been left leaning against the trench wall. Stephen went up and sat beside him.

'Cigarette?' he said.

Douglas nodded. Stephen lit one and put it in Douglas's mouth.

'Help me up,' said Douglas, 'just so I can sit.'

Stephen lifted him further with his arm round his shoulders. Douglas's blood was pumping from a shrapnel wound in his shoulder.

'What's that white on my leg?' he said.

Stephen looked down. 'It's a bone,' he said. 'It's the femur. It's all right, it's just bone. You've lost some muscle.'

Douglas's blood was all over Stephen. It had a peculiar smell, not unpleasant in itself, though cloying in such quantity. It was fresh. It was like the smell in the back of a butcher's shop, only stronger.

'Is Tom all right?' said Douglas.

'Who?'

'Tom Brennan.'

'Yes, I think so. Don't worry, Douglas. Hold on to me. We'll get you some morphine. Try and stop this bleeding. I'm going to put something on your shoulder. It's just a field dressing.'

As he pressed it to the wound he felt Douglas's flesh slipping under his hands. A rib or two had collapsed and his hand was going in towards the man's lung. He stopped the pressure.

'Hunt!' he shouted. 'For Christ's sake get a stretcher here. Get me some morphine.'

Douglas's blood had run up inside the arms of Stephen's uniform. It was on his face and in his hair. His trousers were saturated. Douglas was hanging on to him.

'Have you got a wife, Douglas?'

'Yes, sir.'

'Do you love her?'

'Yes.'

'Good. I'll tell her. I'll write to her. I'll tell her you're the best man we've got.'

'Am I going to die?'

'No, you're not. But you won't be able to write a letter. I'll tell her all the things you did. The patrols and so on. She'll be proud. Where's that morphine? Hunt, for Christ's sake! You love your wife, Douglas. You'll see her again. Think of her when you get to hospital. Hold on to that thought. Don't let go of it. It's all right, it's all right, they're coming. Hold my arm there. That's right. I'm going to take that cigarette or it'll burn you. Don't worry, I'll give you another one. There you are.'

Stephen did not know what he was saying. He was close to choking on Douglas's blood. By the time the stretcher-bearers reached them Douglas had lost consciousness. They levered the inert body up, trying not to make the wound worse.

As they moved off there was a screaming metal sound overhead. Another shell landed with an explosion of light. For a moment Stephen saw the whole line of the trench, straight for twenty yards, then dog-toothed to prevent blast, then straight again. He saw the land behind it stretching out for miles; trees, a distant farmhouse. For an instant it was calm: rural France lay bathed in radiant light.

Then, with the earth and shrapnel flying, he was blown forward. The rear stretcher-bearer had been hit in the head. Douglas lay tipped out on the duckboards. Stephen, unhurt, shouted, 'Get him out. Hunt! Get him out!' Feeling the stickiness on his face, he held his head in his hands and called out, 'Get this man's blood off me.'

Where My Heart Used to Beat

THERE HAD BEEN a place on offer at a London teaching hospital when I graduated from university in June, but it was already clear that there were more pressing events in Europe. My degree meant that I was to become an officer. The NCOs enjoyed humiliating the cadets who nervously lined up on the parade ground of the officer cadet training unit near Doncaster. There was no answer to their greater age and experience; I concentrated on making myself invisible and taking whatever abuse came my way. Once, when a sergeant mocked my slackness at drill – 'You're like a string puppet, not a fucking soldier' – I heard a snigger from a few places down the line. I thought that as a fellow cadet he should have been on my side, not the sergeant's. The fine day came at last when the bullies of the parade ground had to call us 'Sir'. They did it with good grace; they knew there would shortly be other young men to push around.

We were told we were off to France and were kitted out with full uniforms. These included a magnificent overcoat, as well as gas cape and backpack; to the webbing were attached tin helmet, pistol, binoculars, compass, haversack for rations and a water bottle. Once over the Channel, we were sent to a village near Lille, where we were to join the second battalion.

In our billet I first met the officer commanding B Company, a regular called Richard Varian. His moustache was of military cut, but to me it also suggested a French novelist of the belle époque; he carried several books of a non-military nature – poems, biographies – which he arranged on a portable shelf in his room. I had no idea what a commanding officer was supposed to look like. Richard Varian had eyes of such deep brown that they were almost black; he hardly ever seemed to blink. I thought I saw kindness there as well as intelligence, but it was too soon to be sure.

'You'll be taking over Four Platoon from Bill Shenton,' he said. 'He's been platoon sergeant major for two years. He served with me in India.'

Varian explained that in peacetime there had been a shortage of officers and no need for each platoon to have a subaltern in charge; many had therefore been commanded by such NCOs as Shenton, temporarily promoted. I felt uneasy about replacing a regular when I had never seen action.

'It's your first challenge as an officer,' said Varian, putting a cigarette into his holder. 'I expect there'll be others.'

I found Bill Shenton playing cards in a small scullery

that served as a sergeants' mess. I told him I would like to have a word with him.

'Yes, sir.'

We stood facing one another in the narrow passageway outside, with Shenton standing to attention. He was about ten years older and four inches taller than I was; his face was lined from years of exposure to hot suns. I had met his physical type before on the farms of my childhood, but had never seen a man quite this self-possessed.

'Stand easy,' I said.

I could feel him taking in my youthful, indoor looks. I blushed and lost track of what I was saying in my determination not to break eye contact. I explained that the new arrangement was not my choice, but that I would appreciate his advice from time to time, when I asked for it.

As I brought my fumbling speech to an end, I wondered whether Shenton would burst out laughing or punch me in the jaw.

'I understand, sir.' His face showed no twitch of amusement or anger. He was too loyal to the regiment.

'Thank you, Sergeant Major. You can get back to your game now.'

As he saluted me and turned to leave, it occurred to me that he had probably been told by Varian what was coming, or that he would have deduced it himself from the large intake of young officers. I felt that my inexperience had been taken advantage of by these two regulars: they had wanted to see me go through the motions. On the other hand, for a commanding officer and an NCO respectively, they were promising material.

The men I was commanding were all regulars or reservists. Our job in France was to wait and see what the Germans did; we were not allowed to march into Belgium for fear it might provoke Hitler to invade. As junior officer, I was in charge of the mess and went to discuss food with the cook, Private Dobson, another regular who had come back from India, where he had served in Horse Transport. He told me he had no experience of kitchen work, though he said he'd once helped make a horse curry.

When the Germans, unprovoked, invaded Belgium and the Low Countries in May, we were free to advance at last. Richard Varian issued orders and I was happy to get moving and have a chance to prove myself to the men. Varian took his orders from the battalion commander, who was told what to do by the brigadier. Some said the hierarchy was like Russian dolls; it was more as I imagined a boarding school: the platoon was the class, the company the house and the school itself the battalion. Three battalions, usually from different regiments and counties (say, Yorkshire, Nottinghamshire, Kent), made a brigade, though the brigade, oddly, did not inspire the same sense of belonging as the next larger unit, the division.

My little platoon seemed happy enough, provided they were well fed; and, as we advanced, the Belgians offered cheese, bread and wine, as well as cigarettes and water, to augment our rations. The young women were thrillingly grateful, and I began to feel that soldiering was in my blood – especially when I went out one night to check on the sentries and was accosted by a girl who can't have been more than nineteen. Something about the invasion of her country and the sight of sweating infantry had excited a strong desire in her; we had scarcely been through the pleasantries in broken French before she was kissing me on the lips. Her parents would be away the next day, she said, so if I cared to come by her house, the last one on the left down there . . . I said I thought it would be difficult to get away, but that I would try. What do women want? I asked myself as I returned to my billet. To be kissed in the dark by a soldier. Could that be the answer?

We didn't get far into Belgium before, to our astonishment, we were ordered to withdraw. Six days later, we were marching back through the same village, and when we passed the churchyard I turned my head away in case my girl was there, jeering. Although the German air force attacked our column, we were never forced back by their infantry and I could sense Varian's reluctance to comply with successive orders to withdraw. There was talk of an exposed flank – something I knew from infantry lectures in Doncaster to be a disaster. It turned out to be yet worse, as I discovered one night when I was told to lead a patrol to make contact with the troops on our right. After several confusing hours in a wood, many compass readings and miles of walking, I returned to company headquarters to tell Major Varian that there were no troops on our right. The French, we later heard, had been overrun by German panzer groups to the south, while to the north Holland had capitulated and the Belgians were in full retreat. So it turned out we had both flanks exposed, and were ripe to be cut off and killed, like the Romans at Cannae, as I remembered from the schoolroom.

When we passed through Brussels for the second time I expected to be pelted with rotten vegetables, but the people were forgiving, as they assured us we would be back before long. Third time lucky, maybe. From Lille we marched to Armentières on the bed of a railway, which was difficult, as the sleepers were irregularly placed and the shale slippery. Fortunately, the sky was lit with fire on all sides as we pushed on to Poperinghe.

The names were familiar: these were the lowlands of Flanders where only twenty-five years earlier our fathers had first shaken hands with the twentieth century. And here we were again, under the same faintly absurd name, the 'British Expeditionary Force'.

After marching, there came digging. After digging there came sleep, sometimes, but always more marching. The days had a dreamlike quality. Sometimes when I awoke, I expected to find it had not been real; that I had moved back into a saner existence, like a train switched from a siding to the mainline. One night I lay in the open, with my face turned to the moon, and hoped that a German fighter-bomber would see this pale oval and take pity.

The Germans were certainly indiscriminate. Their

planes swept over the mingled columns of soldiers and refugees, machine guns rattling. Wounded infantry lay on the road beside bleeding children. We had now lost touch with B Echelon – the fancy name for the unit whose job was to carry supplies, water, blankets and officers' valises; I never saw my service dress or new overcoat again. Having no more than the small haversacks and the clothes we stood up in, we collapsed in a wood. Drops of rain soon turned to a pitiless downpour. The men grumbled, but I told them – only guessing and hoping – that the mud would stop the German infantry from advancing and surrounding us.

The battalion received orders to make for the beaches at Dunkirk. With so many refugees on the road, it was impossible to maintain marching order and before we reached the port the men divided into smaller units. I had not seen Richard Varian for two days and the company had become divided; when my platoon arrived at the beach we were told there were no more boats that night, so the men dug holes in the sand to provide cover against the German shelling and bombing. It was a full day later that we scrambled into waiting craft that took us out to a ship. I calculated that B Company had walked a hundred miles in three days. I lay down on the metal deck and woke up in England.

. . .

AFTER DUNKIRK, WE had the task of protecting the British coastline against invasion. My battalion was stationed between Exeter and Lyme Regis and I spent many evenings in the pubs of Seaton, Whimple and Ottery St Mary. We had taken on volunteers, so for the first time I was commanding some men younger than myself and this gave a small lift to my confidence; I felt that even the shambles of Dunkirk now counted as 'action' of a kind. Other subalterns had joined us, and to my delight one of them was Donald Sidwell, who had applied to my regiment despite his mother begging him to join the navy.

There were two others I became friends with at once. John Passmore was a New Zealander who had been brought up in London and become a schoolmaster. He had narrow eyes and dark hair and was extremely left-handed. He was a clever, capable man, rather reserved (I think he liked the formality of the classroom), but, as we discovered, a fine sportsman. The other was a fair-haired giant called Roland Swann, known as 'Vesta', who worked for his family's jute import business in London and was in his late twenties. He had spent some time with a territorial outfit and was very keen to see action; he was always talking about what fun it would be 'when the balloon goes up'. Where Passmore was composed and well dressed, Swann always had a button missing. Although a bachelor himself, he gave matrimonial advice to the men and dictated letters to troublesome wives.

The other notable arrival was Brian Pears, known as 'Fruity', who was a vet in civilian life and through his work with horses had developed an interest in racing and gambling. He was invariably late paying his mess bill, but generous with his occasional winnings. He had the rare gift of speaking German.

While we were in Devon, Bill Shenton put together a cricket team to play the local villages. John Passmore was the best player – a looping left-arm spinner and aggressive number-five batsman. Roland Swann, a clumsy wicket-keeper, was the captain because Passmore was too modest; Brian Pears was an adhesive batsman but unreliable runner between the wickets: 'Yes . . . No . . . Shit!' As Passmore pointed out, '"Shit" does not constitute a call, Brian.'

Bill Shenton was the opening bowler and the near-toothless Private 'Gnasher' Lewis, who was killed in Tunisia, opened from the other end. Connor and McNab, two tough men from the battalion police, were in the middle order and the team was completed by Private Easton, a spinner of sorts, Corporal 'Tall' Storey, a batsman, and Private Hall, a swing bowler who died of his wounds at Anzio.

Kilmington, a village with a wonderful flat pitch and a tall cedar in the corner, set us 240 to win, and we made it. We played a local school, then a club side at Sidmouth, where Shenton hit one over the wall at mid-wicket, across the road and into the sea. One Sunday, when things were quiet, we drove inland to the village of Chardstock, where the pitch is on a steep slope. For weeks afterwards, the men spoke about the tea the opposition had provided, with ham, cheese and fruit from their own farms. I don't remember that we ever lost a game, and this was largely due to John Passmore, whose buzzing left-arm spin took five wickets every time we played.

It sounds more carefree than it can really have been. This was not 1914, after all; we knew what modern war entailed and I was not the only one to have lost a father in the last one. We had no giddy patriotism or hopes of a swift ending; we were angry with the politicians and the diplomats who had once more failed us, worried that Europe would now be at war for ever – a continent doomed by unresolved historical enmities, by the weakness of our leaders and perhaps by the very nature of the species we belonged to.

And yet . . . When I look now, there was a degree of innocence. We were young and hadn't learned the lessons of our fathers: we knew the truth, but didn't feel it. Each man brought his private self to the shared endeavour: 'Gnasher' Lewis, from a small street in Leicester, proud to have been selected for the team, perhaps writing home to his mother with his version of a match report . . . John Passmore, quietly determined to see his wife again, to resume his life in the classroom . . . Private Hall, whose father was a plumber, writing a card to each of his three sisters.

From the present day, it seems obvious which one would have a market stall and which would be a partner in a country law firm – as though character were always destiny. But that was not the case in 1941, when we were still unformed, our quirks not yet hardened into traits. We made little of the differences between us; and one of the things that bound us was the knowledge that machine guns did not discriminate. Shell fragments cared nothing for 'potential'.

The feeling I had for all of these men was pure and undifferentiated. I loved them not for who they were, but for the fact that they were there.

Within a few days of landing in North Africa, we saw all the action any of us could have wanted. It was now April 1943 and there had been many changes. The battalion was commanded by a man called Taylor-West, known to the men as Sailor-Vest or Tightarse. It was his opinion that we were not keen enough, and in a hall near our billet at the Algerian port of Bône he set about giving us a demonstration of how a fighting man should sleep. He lay on a wooden table on his right side, with his rifle gripped in his left hand, the bayonet point by his nose.

'There's no need for anything more than a dry board,' he said. 'Blankets and straw just slow you down. Don't loosen your boots. Two hours is long enough for an officer, three for other ranks. Open your bowels before breakfast each day.'

He began his little talk by saying, 'On the Western Front, when my company overran the Hun at Vimy, we found the machine gunners chained to their guns. Our men were also chained, but by a stronger bond.' He paused and looked at the incredulous faces. 'Loyalty.'

Taylor-West belonged to another regiment and had been dropped on us by the divisional commander. On the face of it, you could see why. He was a regular soldier who had won an MC on the Somme in 1916 and a DSO at Dunkirk – the sort of man you'd want as a battalion commander. His approach to war was simple: kill as many Germans as possible. Some of us had expected that his long experience would have given him some subtler tactical understanding, but his lust for German blood came first. He seemed quite manic with it sometimes.

Richard Varian had been appointed his adjutant and found it hard to conceal his dislike. I suspected that what irked Varian, who enjoyed a cigar and a drink in the mess, was that Taylor-West was a non-smoking teetotaller; I think Varian found something repugnant in a man who could soberly wish to kill so many others. In order not to appear disloyal, Varian began to play a muted part, spending hours on 'liaison'. To the rest of us, this seemed a waste of our best officer.

And our turn had come. Command of B Company had passed from Varian to Vesta Swann, now a captain, and I was his second in command. Donald Sidwell and Fruity Pears commanded A and C Companies respectively; John Passmore was given D. I suspected the reason that I was the last to be promoted was that I was not a public schoolboy, but I was happy to let Swann take the flak from

Taylor-West, while I concerned myself with the morale of the platoon commanders, who were impatient to start fighting.

The Eighth Army had driven the Germans eastward across North Africa. They had been able to use tanks over the level desert sands, but the terrain near Tunis became mountainous. Tanks were no use, and artillery had to be brought up to support the final infantry assault that was meant to remove the Axis powers from Africa for all time.

Our spotters had identified a ridge behind which the big guns could be concealed. The battalion was ordered on to this elevated position, which was less than a mile from the German line. We were only a few hundred yards forward of our own artillery and we had two 25-pounders at our company HQ. Vesta Swann had been bitten by a dog and taken to hospital to have rabies injections, so I found myself in charge of B Company as night fell. We were to occupy the extreme right of the ridge; A Company was in the middle, D on the left and C in reserve.

I had Bill Shenton with me, for which I was grateful, as well as plenty of men I knew from my old platoon. The ground was full of small rocks and stones, and we were not allowed to follow the normal practice of digging in, for fear of making too much noise. So it was that my first close-quarters infantry action entailed me lying beneath the stars, with no comforting walls of earth to flank me, quite unprotected from anything the Hermann Goering

Parachute Division might throw at us. It was not what we'd learned from the infantry rulebook.

This was the strangest moment of my life, yet some low drive in me contrived to make it normal. I thought about the ancient city of Carthage, which had been on the site of present-day Tunis. Its greatest son, Hannibal, had defeated the Romans three times, once, in northern Italy, when he supplied his troops by elephants driven over the Alps. So impressed had the Romans been by Hannibal that they sent Scipio Africanus to confront him, using his own tactics, at Carthage – just a few miles to the east of where I lay with Sergeant Major Shenton, from Accrington, under the same stars.

I told Shenton about Hannibal and he asked me how I knew.

'Livy. The historian.'

'Who?'

'Livy. Titus Livius. He wrote a history of Rome.'

'But this Hannibal was beaten here. In Tunis?'

'Yes, he was. Just over there. Those distant lights. A good omen, don't you think?'

'Maybe. I'd give anything for a smoke.'

'Me too.'

'Do you think the Huns are really watching? They'd see a little light?'

'Probably. May as well get some sleep,' I said.

'On the rocks with my boots on,' said Shenton. 'Tightarse would approve.'

'Don't stick your bayonet up your nose.'

I lay down on the scrubby ground and rested my head on my haversack. I had begun to think about Mr Liddell ringing the bell on the piece of string outside my bedroom door in my last year at school. It must have been the thought of Latin. Then I began to replay very slowly the cricket match at Kilmington in 1941, seeing if I could remember the exact course of events. I was aware that my thought patterns were bizarre, but I supposed it was because I didn't want to inhabit the moment. I could allow my mind to wander for a long period without touching the home ground of self-awareness. War, Tunisia, the stony desert ground, the possibility of imminent death: I absented myself from all that, then wondered what it might be like to think like this always – never to check back with that constant sense of who and where one was. Would a person with such an ability be a genius or a demigod, or simply the village idiot?

Bill Shenton had started to snore and I wondered if it would reach the Germans. I heard the over-praised song of a nightingale, then a loud snapping noise, followed by others. It was a moment before I recognised the sound as rifle fire. I was annoyed that Three Platoon on our extreme right seemed to have opened fire without my order, and I sent a bright nineteen-year-old called Watts to tell them to stop it.

He didn't come back, so ten minutes later, with the noise increasing, I set off with Shenton and two others to find out what was going on. As we rounded a rock on top of the ridge, we saw a group of German soldiers below us in the moonlight. They were advancing, bent double, climbing towards Three Platoon. I knelt down and tried to think.

Our attack was not due for forty-eight hours and was supposed to follow heavy softening-up from our artillery. I would be in trouble with Taylor-West if we precipitated too much action too soon. Little gobbets of infantry wisdom came back to me: reinforce success, if in doubt go forward . . . None of them seemed appropriate. I was aware of a griping pain in my bowels. What on earth am I supposed to do? I must have said this out loud, because Bill Shenton said, 'Kill them, sir.'

I liked it that he remembered to say 'sir'. Unfortunately, I only had a pistol with me, so I told Shenton to throw a grenade. After it had detonated, we saw them scuttling back towards their own line, though one of them lay wounded, possibly dead. These Germans must have been a patrol, or a section that had become detached, because it was a well-organised body of infantry that was attacking Three Platoon, as we discovered when we got there. I ran back and ordered another platoon over to reinforce Three, which still left me with enough men to stay in touch with A Company in the middle of the ridge.

Rifle and machine-gun fire was starting up all along our line. There was no time for discretion any more and I felt relieved; if the Hun was coming, let him come. I resumed my original position with Shenton beside me and organised our defences as best I could. It was difficult to see the enemy by night, and we had to fire in the direction of a flash or a sound. I ordered some of the men to start digging pits for the Bren guns and told the lieutenant, a new arrival called Bell, to send for more ammunition. After about two hours, it became clear that the worst had happened and the enemy had got in behind us. My company was now under fire on three sides and there was nothing our artillery behind us could do; our only hope was that C Company might be sent up from reserve. The radio had broken down, so I sent a runner to battalion headquarters to explain our plight.

'They've got a machine-gun post up there, behind that rock,' Shenton yelled at me. 'We've got to get rid of it.'

'How the fuck did they get in there?'

'We're strung out too thin. I'll go if you like, sir.'

'I'll come too. Get three others you trust. We'll use grenades. All right?'

'Yes. Then rifles and bayonets when we get in close.'

I couldn't see which three men he'd got. Their faces were blacked and I didn't want to know. We set off, Shenton leading, over the scrub and stones. There was some sort of hut, possibly a shepherd's shelter, from which the enemy machine guns were firing towards A Company on our left.

We got as close as we could, behind some thorny bushes. The three men knelt down beside us, panting in the dim moonlight.

'On the word "go", we just charge,' I said. 'Is that right, Sergeant Major?'

'Yes, sir.'

My mouth was so dry I had to lick my lips before I could speak. 'Nothing fancy,' I said. 'As fast as you can. Throw your grenades and keep running.'

The machine gun started up again. Under the cover of its noise I gave the word, and we set off. After three years of physical training, we were quick over the ground, even that treacherous, dark surface. When I estimated we were twenty-five yards short, the furthest I could accurately lob, I threw my grenade and the others followed suit. We kept running and, as the bombs went off, made it round the side of the hut. We came in from behind and began to fire on those still standing. There were a dozen men in there, only three or four of whom had been disabled by the blast of the grenades. The rest we killed. I don't know who did what, I can't remember. You are not yourself at such a time. We lost one man in the attack and I gave the order to get back to our line at once. We would find and bury him the next day.

The journey back was quick and the enemy fire came close only once. I lay down by my haversack, gasping. There was blood on my bayonet and I wiped it on a bush. A messenger came to say the Germans had driven tanks past the right end of the ridge. I sent more men to defend our right flank, where some were now forced to fire towards our own lines.

We could only fight on. There was nothing else to do. While they still came for us it showed that the ridge was important to them, that the war had not passed us by. I went round encouraging the men, though I could see the fatigue in their eyes.

Time seemed to slow and hang heavy in the noise of guns. I felt if I closed my eyes I might sleep for ever. But this was battle and at least I had not yet disgraced myself, I thought, as I trained my field glasses on the ground behind us. It was starting to grow light and I saw what I thought must be C Company under Brian Pears coming towards the ridge. Word must have got through. But their progress was impeded by the German tanks and infantry that had outflanked us. Behind them I could see British tanks starting to manoeuvre and within twenty minutes a counter-attack had begun. It was a wonderful sight. Tanks reminded me of Hannibal's elephants, cumbersome, thick-skinned, spitting fire from their long trunks. I saw a flash from one and watched a German tank explode before the noise of either detonation reached me.

An hour later, Brian Pears arrived with the battalion water cart. We had had nothing to drink for a day.

'I had you at six-to-four against holding on here,' said Pears. 'I suppose I'll have to pay up now. The counter-attack's gone well. The Hun's thrown in the sponge.'

'Nice of you to turn up,' I said.

In the morning light, I could see an old mosque about half a mile west on the ridge. It had been occupied by

Germans, and I suggested to the gunnery officer that he might hit it with a 25-pounder. It was an adventure for him to see his target, as he was normally so far back that he fired according to wireless or telephone direction from a forward spotter.

He seemed at first reluctant to have his accuracy so nakedly tested, but eventually fired a single shell. There was a whine and a juddering and then the mosque fell in with a roar, disgorging a dozen Germans with their hands up and, at the end of this dusty line, a relieved Gnasher Lewis, whom they had captured.

By noon the Germans were in full retreat, leaving behind scores of dead and wounded in the plain and on the ridge. The battle pushed on to the east, but we had done what had been asked of us. The battalion, shaken and dust-covered, was still in place. I went to visit my platoons, to check on the casualties.

To my delight, I saw poppy fields on the other side of the slope; then by an olive tree I found the body of nineteen-year-old Private Watts, whom I had sent to his death. Such was the cost of appearing 'bright'. We buried him beneath the tree and stuck his bayonet and rifle in the ground with his helmet on the butt. I gathered half a dozen men and read the funeral service, a copy of which I had in my pocketbook.

The casualties were lighter than I had feared from the intensity of the assault. We had killed enough Germans to satisfy even Taylor-West and had taken twice that number prisoner. It was beyond doubt a victory, a hard-fought one at that, but I felt no exhilaration. When, under Lieutenant Bell, the men were safely on their way back to battalion headquarters, I knelt down behind a rock and wept.

A few months after the battle in Medjez Plain, I found myself standing among hundreds of men packed into a troopship's muster area. During the voyage up from Salerno, I had been able to spend much of the day on deck; it was cold up there in the winter wind, but at least the air was fresh and there were things to look at through my field glasses: the docks of Naples, packed with Allied shipping; the crown of Vesuvius preparing to erupt. For the last few hours, though, since we had come within range of German artillery and bombers, we had been confined to a space below decks where there was no room to sit down except on the metal floor.

In our last week in Tunisia, Taylor-West had been wounded while leading a patrol (something he was not supposed to do); on returning from hospital in Algiers he was detailed to join a commando training school in Scotland, and Richard Varian was promoted colonel and given command of the battalion. The morale of the men seemed to lift at once; it felt as if the king across the water had been restored.

An odour of vomit mixed with the smell of unwashed men as the ship pitched on the winter swell. I was standing a few inches from a steel bulkhead, at whose paintwork

I was staring under the strip light. On warships, paint is the only upholstery; nothing else is thought necessary to separate flesh from metal. I wondered as I gazed at the rivets and flanges, painted and repainted by some able seaman on fatigues, whether Donald Sidwell's mother would really have wished him to spend five years like this. Casualties at sea might have been fewer than in the infantry, but at least we had seen villages and woods, sand and stars.

If we couldn't be on deck, my remedy against seasickness was to breathe deeply and hold the air in the lungs. By now I could feel the cold sweat on my scalp and the tingling sensation in feet and hands that mean the moment is near. I had always thought it odd that such a trivial complaint should feel so deathly.

The day before, as we steamed north of Naples, Richard Varian gave a talk to the men of our battalion. We were called together at 0900 hours on B deck and told to stand easy.

Varian looked confident and clear-eyed. He wore a well-ironed battledress with a cream scarf at his neck.

'You'd probably like to know what's going on,' he said. 'Though I know you've all heard rumours. The truth is quite dramatic enough. We're going to make a surprise landing about an hour south of Rome by road, at a seaside town called Anzio. There are twenty-seven battalions going in. That's roughly fifty thousand men. Our aim is to be in Rome in less than two weeks.'

There was some muttering from the men. They were clearly proud to have been given such a task, but daunted, too. They knew the Germans by now. Varian waited for the noise to die down.

'All right,' he said. 'A little bit of background. Forgive me if I'm teaching my grandmother . . . But some of you won't know this. Since last September, the Americans and some of our chaps have been battering their way up the boot of Italy – up mountains, over rivers, down coastal plains, facing an enemy who've always had the high ground. And nowhere more so than at Cassino, which is about ninety miles south-east of Anzio, where the Germans hold a monastery on a hilltop and the Allied advance has come to a halt.'

He glanced round to see if they were still following. 'Our landing at Anzio will give us the back door to Rome. The enemy will have to move reinforcements up from Cassino and this will enable us to break through there at last. When we push out of the beachhead, we'll join the Americans coming up from the south. Then we can outflank the Germans, take large numbers of prisoners and march on to Rome without too much resistance.'

Varian coughed and looked down at his notes for a moment. 'Of course,' he said, 'it's a risky operation, but it's more than a stunt. Our leaders are certain that the loss of Rome will be a blow to German pride. This means that when the second front opens – yes, I know you're all sick of hearing about it, but it will happen one day . . . When the Allies do finally land in northern Europe, wherever it may be, the enemy will be demoralised. The Italian campaign – our campaign – is not just a sideshow, a tactic to divert German troops from France. It's vital in its own right. You are the first fighting men to take back occupied Europe from the Nazis. You should be proud.'

Here he paused to give the men a moment to congratulate themselves. The odd thing about Richard Varian was that with his cigars and his poetry books and his light, sardonic manner, he seemed detached from the business of war. Yet soldiering was his profession. He had been embarrassed by the award of the DSO in Tunisia, accepting it, he told us, only as recognition of the battalion's efforts; but we had seen enough of him in action to think it was deserved.

'We expect strong resistance,' he said, 'but look at it this way. Isn't it better to be fighting here, alongside men you've been with for years, than starting guerrilla warfare in Burma, like the poor old Third Battalion? I can guarantee you will also have much better rations. We'll be fighting with the Americans, and you know what that means. Food. The terrain where we establish our beachhead tonight is a reclaimed marsh, between the coast and the inland mountains. It may be wet, but it will be flat, and B Echelon will never be far behind us.'

Our regiment were known as big eaters, so such news always cheered them. Richard Varian ended with the traditional appeal to the regiment's history, including the

Peninsular Wars, and to the courage, discipline and fellowship of the men.

Roland Swann grabbed my sleeve as we dispersed. 'Brace yourself,' he said. 'Richard never appeals to the regiment unless they expect heavy casualties.'

Afterwards, there was a more detailed briefing for the Five Just Men (Varian's name for Sidwell, Pears, Swann, Passmore and me) and each company's second in command. This took place in his cabin and was an informal occasion with whisky and cigarettes.

'Now then. This Italian adventure.' Varian poured himself a refill. 'Entirely between ourselves and not a whisper outside this cabin, but I'm getting a whiff of staff cock-up. Of Gallipoli. These joint operations . . . I don't know. I've nothing against the Americans, but they have their own priorities. And their General Clark seems prone to get the wind up. There are far too many chiefs in my view. It's all come down from Allied command, from the politicians. You can tell that when they talk about a "blow to German pride". That's a politician's idea of a battle, not a soldier's. Our objectives are more complicated than in Tunisia and will depend on communication and good timing. And of course the biggest factor of all. Which is?'

We all knew. Luck.

'Having shared the Jeremiah stuff,' Varian went on, 'let me say that as long as we can break out of the beachhead quickly, we'll be all right. Otherwise . . . I hope you've got some good trench diggers. We expect strong retaliation, so you'll have to dig fast. The terrain also means we could be fighting at close quarters.'

'And if we do end up being there a long time, sir?' said Brian Pears.

'Then we'll draw on all our resources, we'll think again. But communication will be the key. Think ahead. Make sure the radio is always working.'

'First time for everything,' said Passmore.

'All right,' said Varian. 'Point taken. Try and get a back-up set.'

'When we're dug in,' said Donald Sidwell, 'would you like me to lead a patrol to see how far back the enemy line is?'

Richard Varian lit a cigarette and sat back in his chair. 'My dear Donald,' he said, 'are you mad?'

As we were leaving, Varian said, 'One moment, Hendricks.'

I waited till the others had gone.

'Another drink?'

'Thank you. Just a small one.' I had never been keen on whisky, but I knew it was a privilege.

'Once we've established our position in the beach-head,' said Varian, 'I'm putting Nichols in charge of base company. That means I'll need an adjutant. Do you fancy having a go? There'd be a promotion to major.'

'I wouldn't want to leave Major Swann alone in charge of the landings, sir.'

'You don't have to. Help him get B Company ashore and

dug in. Then he can have Bell as his second in command. Bell's a good man, isn't he?'

'Certainly.'

'Don't look so suspicious, Robert. It's quite normal to move people round in wartime. But I want to leave the company commanders as they are. And don't worry if you think you're going to miss any action. We won't. There'll be enough action to go round.'

I thought about Varian's offer as I stood among the pale, retching men below decks. It had become a matter of pride for me not to throw up myself, but I could tell by the sweating and tingling that I didn't have long left. Surely they must let us up soon or we wouldn't have time to get on to the landing craft. Perhaps death by bullet would be less drawn out, less relentlessly unpleasant than this awful . . .

A whistle blew, somebody shouted. There was a stampede of hobnails.

Up on deck, the night seemed dark after the strip lights below. When I had breathed deeply for a minute or so, I looked about and could just see behind us the shapes of hulking warships with their guns raised, waiting for the signal to fire. Such sights you see in naval dockyards or in photographs; I'd never expected to witness them in action – in reality. I thought of all the planning and the navigation it had taken to have these leviathans aligned exactly to the will of a distant politician, now presumably in bed.

For the first time, I had a sense of how many vessels were in our silent armada. Minesweepers had gone ahead to clear the channels for the frigates and destroyers I had just made out; nearer to us on the troopships were smaller vessels that had been protecting the convoy, as well as hundreds of landing craft. I was reassured by the size of our force, by the solid steel of our shipping; but if this was the weight of our sledgehammer, with fifty thousand men waiting to go ashore, then the nut that we were preparing to crack must be . . .

Breathing in again, I decided not to think about the enemy. I pictured instead the Italian inhabitants of the town and its surroundings, whose lives had only a few minutes of relative tranquillity left to run: sleeping children, two or three to a wooden bed; grandmothers in their widow's black; farmers who had already yielded their meagre harvests to the enemy; boatbuilders and peasants . . . Who else might scrape a living from the edges of the marsh? Now Jupiter Omnipotens was about to unleash his thunderbolts on the plain of Latium.

We went down nets into the landing craft. The air was filled with voices calling, radios crackling, shouts of 'B Company here!' or 'Fourteen to the stern!' as men tried to find the right boat and their own platoon.

At such moments in the war so far, I had always thought first of my own safety. I wondered if it might be possible to go through the motions of fighting without exposing myself to danger – to advance behind the shoulder of Bill

Shenton or some other big fellow; to accidentally turn an ankle; to be the first to duck, the last to leave the shelter of a slit trench or bombed villa . . . As a veteran of Dunkirk and North Africa, I could trade reminiscences with Richard Varian and his company commanders, rub shoulders with the men, make sardonic jokes about the radio – then hide. With an amphibious assault there would be such chaos that anyone who simply ducked and ran wouldn't be noticed. That's what my mother would have recommended. And then I had an image of her asleep in her bedroom at the Old Tannery, her hair in some night-time net or curlers, her face against the pillow, clenched in shallow, unrelaxing sleep. I could almost smell the winter damp of the garden, hear the dripping cedar by the wall. It was a place that seemed not so much distant as unreal. The cold wind that blew against my cheek and the metal deck that rose beneath my feet could not belong in the same universe as her bedroom.

Some of the men were silently praying. I looked at their bowed heads and saw their lips move. Not one of them was by temperament suited for what lay ahead. No child is born a soldier: not Storey, Hall, McNab, Jones, Rutherford or any of the rest whose blackened faces I strained to recognise. In that moment, I saw that my own fear was no worse than theirs and told myself to do whatever needed to be done. The worst that waited for me was a bullet or a shell, then death in the January shallows. If I was ready to accept that possibility and go on, then in return the god

Some of the men were silently praying. I looked at their bowed heads and saw their lips move. Not one of them was by temperament suited for what lay ahead. No child is born a soldier.

of war, or whatever lunatic was in charge, would surely make it quick. And that was my version, I suppose, of ‘leadership’.

The shoreline lit up. There was sand leaping, trees and houses lifting from the ground. We heard the air above fill with the rockets fired from the landing craft nearby and the howling of the bigger guns far out at sea. Earth, sky and water were fused orange; as if on cue, there came the rumble of distant bombing over the Alban Hills. I felt a throb of elation at the thought of the bomber pilots in their freezing cockpits, their navigators, bomb aimers and tail gunners, raising gloved thumbs-up at the end of their run from whatever distant base. I loved those men up in the icy air. Oh God, perhaps we would still do this, put an end to the meat-grinding and swoop to some final victory. Then I felt pity for the enemy beneath our bombardment – their skulls crashing and bones blown out.

For a moment there was silence, as though time couldn’t move. But in this war it seemed there was always someone, usually an engineer, doing something you knew nothing about, and there was no escape, only a forward momentum through the swell. So the boats were moving.

It was difficult to make out where we were going except when the shore was lit by our rockets and shells, but the pilots seemed to know and the boats ploughed on. When we were perhaps two hundred yards out, the enemy gun batteries responded at last. Men around me crouched down on the metal floor of our boat, holding their helmets down with both hands, as though this might help. The iron flanks of the landing craft echoed and rattled with the explosion of German shells in the water. As the hull hit the sand, we pitched forward on to one another, fell and staggered and stood. The front of the craft was let down with a splash. I knew that some of the men couldn't swim, so I was anxious to make sure the sea was no more than waist deep. Some unfortunate boat had run aground on a sandbar in the deep and I guessed only the swimmers had survived. 'Keep your rifles dry!' I remembered to shout as I jumped in. I had never known sea so cold, and with the weight of my pack and the soft sand under my feet, it came to the armpits. For a second I had some absurd memory of Bexhill-on-Sea, childhood, the taste of salt . . . Then, roaring in protest against the icy water, I pushed on into the shallows, where the corpses of two young men were rolling, tumbling playfully back and forth.

We followed a white tape through a minefield on the beach and regrouped at a half-destroyed building beside the road. The men were shivering and wet, but elated at having come this far alive. Some made jokes about swallowing water and doing the breaststroke. 'It's colder than bloody Bridlington,' said Hall.

By now there were German bombers overhead as well as artillery fire from the direction of Rome, but as yet there seemed to be no ground troops. Knowing the enemy as we did, we guessed they were waiting for a better moment to attack. We feared a trap. There were too many of our own troops on the one metalled road and it was hard for men to find their units. Eventually, I had gathered those I was supposed to be with and, after some torch and compass work, we set off across the fields towards the Moletta River. I had Three Platoon with me and was told by Vesta Swann to lead the way to our first objective, an improbably distant farmhouse. This was what all company commanders seemed to do: delegate at once, don't go yourself, but show your commitment and aggressive intent by sending your second in command with his best men. Private Hall was our champion map reader, so I put him in front with Sergeant Warren and half a dozen others whose wariness and stamina I trusted.

There were burning buildings in the stubble fields where icy puddles cracked beneath our feet. We expected every barn or haystack to conceal an ambush, so went at a steady pace, rifles at the ready. I said nothing to the men, but by now I was certain we had caught the enemy by surprise. As I looked left towards the sea to get a bearing, I saw one of our ships – a frigate, I think – on fire in the bay and it filled me with an awful melancholy, more than the sight of burning flesh.

The pace slowed as we entered thick pine woods; by the time we emerged, it was starting to grow light: a smear over dun-coloured marsh. My boots had let in seawater, but in the course of the night had let most of it out again. The plodding over heavy ground through dripping woods was what we had been trained to do, and though my neck and shoulders ached, my legs were still willing.

I conferred with Hall and Warren. Through my field glasses I could see our objective: a two-storey, blue-painted farmhouse, one of hundreds built as part of Mussolini's project to reclaim the marsh for agriculture. We took another map reading to be sure. I was keen to get there before full daylight, so after a five-minute rest, we moved on at the double.

A hundred yards short of the house, we aimed some mortar rounds at the front as a distraction, while I sent a patrol of six led by Bill Shenton to go round the back. Within five minutes a flare went up to tell us it was all clear. Inside the house they had a three-generation Italian family of ten lined up in the living room and four Germans taken prisoner.

I took Private Hall upstairs, and in a sort of hayloft we found two more Germans asleep. Hall prodded them awake with his rifle butt and we dragged them out. They looked appalled as we pushed them along the candle-lit passage, but by the time we had got them downstairs their faces were beginning to show a furtive relief. I ordered Corporal Parfitt, a Wearsider I trusted, and two others from the platoon to take the Germans back to base. It was an awful task, really, to tramp over the same ground, but at least it saved them the digging-in that awaited the rest of us. I watched these somnolent German men walk out of the war with a sense of raging envy.

Bill Shenton was smashing out the windows and organising men to fill sandbags, while the Italian women wept at the desecration of their home. I told them in my rough Italian to be quiet and make some food. '*Piano, piano, per favore . . . Inglesi molto gentili . . . Tutto bene, no lacrima . . . Mangiare . . . Pasta, formaggio, zuppa . . . presto, presto.* Come on, come *on*! *Domani, voi . . .*' I smiled and pointed back towards the port, to suggest that tomorrow we would safely evacuate them. '*Tutto bene per voi.*'

A woman of about forty, presumably the mother of the house, seemed to understand and went reluctantly towards the kitchen. A signals unit was meanwhile moving in with a radio to make an observation post upstairs, in the room where Hall and I had routed out the sleepers.

At about ten o'clock I was joined by Vesta Swann, who had been clearing out stragglers, as he put it, from some farm buildings along the way. He looked tired, the skin stretched tight over his large, blank face, but I was happy to hand over command to him of what had become known after its former occupants as 'The Dormitory'.

In the evening of the first day, we established contact with Richard Varian, who was still at the port. He told Swann that the landings had achieved almost complete surprise. Our four companies were all in their allotted places, and apart from some men feared drowned, casualties had been slight. B Echelon was within striking distance and we could expect rations to come up within a few hours.

'I expect we shall then receive orders to advance rapidly,' said Varian. 'Get what rest you can.'

'We're on the end of some mortar and rocket fire now,' said Swann, 'so the enemy must be getting reinforcements.'

'Of course,' said Varian. 'That's why we'll need to move quickly. And if the Yanks hang about, we'll go it alone.'

. . .

THE IDEA THAT you are winning or that 'victory' is soon to be yours was one I'd learned always to distrust. For perhaps twenty-four hours in the Dormitory, however, as we filled sandbags, dug defences, took in a ration party, it was possible to think that at least the plan had not gone wrong yet. I could even spare a section to help one of our mobile artillery pieces to set up and another to help the engineers lay tracks over the boggy ox-cart paths. I enjoyed these housekeeping exercises because I knew they wouldn't last.

That night we came under fire from mortars and rifle grenades. We were well enough placed to repel it, but I thought it was worryingly close at hand. Donald Sidwell's idea of leading a patrol to find out just how near the Germans were seemed not so mad after all. At dawn the next day, Richard Varian arrived by Jeep and told us the Dormitory would now become battalion headquarters.

'And where will B Company headquarters be?' said Vesta Swann.

'That's up to you. A suitable building in Aprilia. Up that

way.' He pointed towards the enemy line. 'The division's going to attack. We can't wait any longer for the Americans while the enemy gets his reinforcement in place. In my view we could almost have been in Rome by now.'

Varian seemed pleased that the British were going it alone, and wanted our battalion to be prominent in the attack. He spoke to Sidwell, Pears and Passmore by radio, then told Vesta Swann that he had appointed me his adjutant, to replace Nichols.

I felt uneasy as I watched Bill Shenton organising the men of Three Platoon that night; I ought to have been blacking up to go with them. As I wished them good luck, Shenton muttered to me, 'Perhaps he doesn't know what a fighter you are.' 'Don't worry, Bill,' I said, 'it's not like a staff job. We'll all be in action soon enough.' But I was touched by his words; it seemed a long time ago that I had had to relieve him of his command on our first day in France.

While there was still time, I managed to get the Italian family on to an empty Bedford OY lorry going back to the port. God knows how they would get out of there with the Luftwaffe bombing anything that moved, but that was not my concern. Perhaps they could wait it out in a friend's cellar. Private Jones, whom I had told to clean the small room they had been packed into, came out with two books they had left behind. One was a popular novel, the other appeared to be a journal; from the handwriting I guessed it belonged to the teenage daughter. I could understand almost nothing of it but put it in my pack in the vague hope of returning it to her one day. I often found myself making plans for reunions and revisits in a future peace – even in the chaos of Belgium and Tunis I had met people I would have wished to see again.

One of the advantages of being adjutant to the commanding officer was the access to food and drink. Some officers liked to build up a stock of whisky, some had a party the moment they received their ration; others, I was pretty sure, kept it for the moment before an attack. Richard Varian liked to keep his level steadily topped up, though he had a rule about the sun being over the yardarm – which was no later than five in an Italian January.

'Do you get any letters, Robert?' he said, splashing whisky into an enamelled mug.

'My mother sends me cuttings from the *Illustrated London News*.'

'Do you have brothers and sisters?'

'No.'

'Girlfriends?'

'No. Well, that's not quite true. There are two girls who write occasionally, Mary and Paula. But they're just friends.'

Varian raised an eyebrow. He looked as groomed as ever, well shaved, his hair and moustache exactly trimmed.

'Do you speak other languages?' I said. It was an odd question, but the conversation was making me feel uneasy.

For one thing I could never bring myself to call him 'Richard' at off-duty moments, as I knew I should.

'I speak Italian fairly well. Schoolboy French and German. I can understand some Hindi and some Urdu from my time out there. You?'

'Nothing helpful. Only dead languages. Latin and Greek. I was studying medicine before I joined up.'

'So you're going to be a doctor?'

'I thought so. But the training's very long. And after all this . . .'

We looked round the small back parlour that Varian had claimed as his headquarters. He lit a candle and poured more whisky.

'Yes,' said Varian. 'After all this . . . It's going to be a bit tame, isn't it?'

'I don't know how I'm going to reconcile what I've seen in the last four years with what I knew before.'

Varian smiled. 'Some days I expect to find myself back in my parents' house in Northumberland, and to discover it's all been a misunderstanding. When I wake up, I look round at the billet, try to remember where the hell it is . . . Listen for gunfire . . . Bombs . . . I give it a chance to shake down and become normal. But if after a minute it's still war, I give in and call my batman. Face another day.'

In truth, it was all very odd. I suppose the fields over which our fathers had fought the Battle of the Somme had for thousands of years between simple farmland, cultivated by smallholders for sugar beet or whatever crop the soil supported. No nineteenth-century ploughman as he turned his great-grandfather's earth thought that one day his field beneath its flat sky would be a second Golgotha.

The land round the Dormitory was almost nondescript, yet I felt sure this nowhere place was about to gain a savage notoriety. Being at the junction of three routes to the front, we could see men coming back from the line. Some were walking, some were going to play no further part and some, shell victims, were bits of human only just cohering on a piece of stretched webbing or a plank. One of them, alas, was Private Hall.

Richard Varian was growing agitated. One evening he laid a map on the table and updated it as best he could with the positions of our companies. 'You know what we've got here, Robert?' he said, drawing a bulge with a pencil. 'We've got a fucking salient.'

I had never heard him swear before.

'Really?'

'Yes. It's like Ypres. Remember that?'

'Not personally,' I said.

'But you know what a salient is?'

'Yes, when you have a perimeter line bent to go round a town or a wood, it's a bit that sticks out, like a . . . like a –'

'Sore thumb. And it can be snipped off, like a thumb, by scissors at the base.'

'Painful.'

'Extremely.'

‘And that’s where B Company is?’

‘That’s my understanding,’ said Varian. ‘The Foresters are up there, too. Good men. And the Duke of Wellington’s. Splendid chaps. The radio’s a bit . . .’

‘In and out?’

‘Yes. And it’s extremely noisy. It’s pretty constant. As you can hear.’

‘Where did all these German troops come from?’ I said.

‘God knows. But you can be sure that Kesselring had a back-up plan. By now they’ll have had time to get more men down from France. Brian Pears says that in six days his men have taken prisoners from eight different divisions.’

‘That’s quite a scramble.’

‘Yes. If we’d moved faster they wouldn’t have had the time.’

Varian sat down. It was the first time I’d seen him at a loss. ‘Which of the company commanders has been longest without a break?’

‘Donald Sidwell,’ I said. ‘Passmore was wounded, Pears had two weeks out before we set sail and Swann missed some of the action in Tunisia.’

‘Hmm. Poor Sidwell. How’s he going to be, do you think? He’s an old pal of yours, isn’t he?’

I smiled. I was thinking of Donald standing up to canter on a broken-winded nag we’d found him, shouting, ‘God this is fun!’ or lecturing me through his thick glasses about Bach.

‘He’ll be fine,’ I said. ‘He’s a man of parts. Did you know

he's very keen on horse racing, among other things? He's probably got some complicated bet going with Fruity Pears about whose company will get furthest.'

Varian puffed at a cigar for a moment. 'I'd like a full report on conditions up there. I've half a mind to go myself.'

'Why don't we get John Passmore to send a few men from D Company?'

'Because,' said Varian, 'I've decided I'm going to send the whole of D Company up as reinforcements anyway. I want you to go with them, then find Sidwell and tell him from me that he's to come back for two weeks' rest.'

'Couldn't one of Passmore's men tell him?'

'No. You're the adjutant. You represent me. If I send a runner, I'm afraid Donald'll just tell him to bugger off.'

'And who'll take over from him?'

'Townsend, his second in command. I need a full report. All right?'

It was an awful journey. We were all supposed to know what we were doing by now, four and a half years into this war, but when you had to go and give a message, well . . . It was a walk, like every other walk I'd ever made – to the station, to the shop, to the farm, to wherever I wanted to go. It was me on my feet plodding over the earth, hoping I was going the right way.

I knew what Richard Varian had meant when he talked about waiting for reality to shake down – and only when it refused to do so would he reluctantly accept . . . One more step forward. If it had been me alone, I would have lain beneath a tree and offered myself up to die, to sleep . . . But there were others there. And for them I was compelled against my will to go through this fatigue, beyond exhaustion, as other men did, and had before, the hoplites at Marathon or the legionaries of Caesar on this same benighted marsh.

A Company headquarters was in a shepherd's hut they had dug out and expanded. In front of it was a scene almost familiar to me: trench warfare. There were sandbags and rolls of barbed wire; there were shattered trees and burned-out vehicles; there were shell holes, dead cattle and live rats. The difference between Anzio and Armentières was that here the water table was so high that no trench was more than three feet deep. I splashed through the mud and excrement of the laughably named 'communication' trench to get to the forward platoon, where I was told I could find Donald. I saw him half sitting, half lying in a pool of water, his spectacles smeared with mud.

I knelt down beside him.

'Christ, look what the cat dragged in.' He couldn't stop a smile from creeping over his face. 'I'm trying to organise some sheep to walk over towards that wood. I think there's a minefield, so I want the sheep to go first. Then if we can get into the wood, we'll have some cover.'

'But aren't the Germans in the wood?'

'The Hun's bloody everywhere. We've got to turf him out. Hence Operation Sheep May S.G.'

'S.G.?'

'Safely Graze. It's a Bach cantata, you ignorant medic.'

'Not so safely, in fact.'

'We hope for the best. Got a man called Sheppard – of all things – who claims he worked on a farm and can drive them across. Bloody dangerous because he'll have to stand up.'

For some reason, I started to laugh. I lay down in the mud and shook with mirth. I was tired. 'Oh, Donald, you really are . . .'

The shells continued to fall and the mortars to crack and plop in the earth behind us.

When I had got control of myself, I said, 'I bring you good tidings.'

'Oh, really? I wondered to what I owed the honour of a visit from the adjutant.'

'You're to go back to the Dormitory, then to B Echelon for a rest. Varian's orders.'

'Good God. Who's going to take over? You?'

'No. Townsend.'

'Christ. Not that clown.'

'That's the order. You're to return at once.'

'Does Varian think I've gone bomb-happy or something?'

'No, but he's aware you've had no time off.'

'It's all a bit odd, Robert. Why me?'

'Because you've been in this hellhole for ten days and you've had not one day off since we landed in North Africa. Because Richard wants you in good shape for what lies ahead.'

'Well, I don't want to leave these men in the lurch, you know. They're a rough bunch, A Company, but –'

'Always were.'

'But they're good. I've got the right men in the right platoons. It's taken years. They'd die for each other now. I can't leave them here. Just look.'

I looked: exhausted soldiers lying in the slurry, exposed, while the enemy regrouped for another attack.

'Better off out of it,' I said.

'What if I say no?'

'Richard'll just send me back with some military police. I don't want to make this journey again.'

'I'll go and speak to Townsend. But I want it recorded that I'm doing this against my will. Under protest.'

When Donald and I eventually got back to the Dormitory, it was to find Sergeant Warren from my own company, B, standing at attention outside the door.

'What the hell are you doing here, Warren? Why aren't you with the rest of the company?'

'Major Swann sent me back, sir.'

'For Christ's sake. What for?'

'Laying down my arms, sir.'

'What the fuck are you talking about?'

'I'm not fighting any more, sir. I told Major Swann so and he sent me back under guard.'

Warren was one of our better men and I should have been considerate, or persuasive, but for some reason – perhaps simple fatigue – I found myself shouting at him.

'Do you know what this means, Warren? You'll be on a charge.'

'Yes, I know that, sir.'

'Desertion? Is that what you want your family to hear? What about all your friends? Are you just going to drop them, leave them in the lurch?'

'I've done all I can do, sir.'

'There are men lying in their own excrement up there, living in a trench two feet deep.'

'I was one of them, sir. And I was in Tunisia. And the Low Countries before that. I've been wounded twice. I've not been a quitter. But I know how far I can go and this is it. I can't take no more. Stick me in prison. I don't mind. I'll take the shame. No man should have to –'

'Be quiet, Warren. Other men have been through more. What about that little boy Watts I sent out to die? He was nineteen. Never even had a night out. Or Travis, who lost both his legs on a mine and dragged himself half a mile back on his stumps.'

'I don't care about Travis, sir. I'm finished.'

'In the last war, you'd have been shot. Taken out at dawn in front of a firing squad of your own men, tied to a tree and shot.'

'I know. But it's prison now.'

'That won't be any better. You'll be in solitary. The guards'll spit at you. Spit in your food. You'll have no friends, none of the laughter, the companionship.'

'I don't want it. I've done my bit. Four years. I've done all I can do.'

'Stay there. Don't move.'

I found Richard Varian upstairs at the observation post. He was looking through his field glasses towards the remote wood – the place of shelter that Donald had wanted. Even with my bare eyes I could see smoke rising. I wondered if Sheppard had ever got his flock across the minefield.

I explained the problem with Warren, but Varian seemed distracted. 'At least he hasn't shot himself in the foot.'

The radio operator said, 'A Company permission to withdraw and dig in further back, sir.'

'Half of bloody Germany's arrived,' said Varian. 'It'll be the Prussian cavalry next.'

'Shall I send Warren to Brigade, sir?' I said.

Varian put down the field glasses. 'I dare do all that may become a man; who dares do more is none,' he said.

'What does that mean?'

'Macbeth. A man may have limits. I don't want to waste manpower getting him back to Brigade. Put him on fatigues for the time being. Pumping out the trenches, filling sandbags, anything you like.'

The radio operator said, ‘We’ve lost contact with A Company, sir.’

It was a long night. The noise of the German artillery and bombers overhead made it difficult to sleep.

Just after dawn, I was woken by my batman, Private Winter. ‘Runner, sir. From D Company. Maybe you should wake the colonel, too.’

‘Why?’

‘Man’s got a message. Says it’s urgent. Doesn’t look good.’

I found Richard Varian already awake in the main downstairs room, holding a piece of paper.

‘It’s from John Passmore,’ he told me. ‘You know he’s tucked in just behind the salient?’

‘Yes.’

He handed me the paper. ‘Regret inform you A Company overrun. All dead or taken prisoner. Have ordered emergency withdrawal of D to agreed position.’

Varian stared at the distant wood.

‘The whole lot,’ he said eventually. ‘Every man gone.’

I didn’t know what to say. This was beyond my experience.

The three of us stood for a long time in silence in the parlour of the Italian farm.

Eventually Varian spoke, in a low, hoarse tone. ‘You can never re-form them. Not when this happens. We’ll be a battalion with no A Company.’

The runner dragged the sleeve of his battledress across his nose.

What had Donald said? 'I've got the right men in the right platoons. They'd die for each other now.'

I wondered how I was going to tell him.

Richard Varian released me from my duties as adjutant. It had become a question of holding on with bleeding nails to stop ourselves being driven back into the sea by the ceaseless bombing and shelling; there was little in the way of 'tactics' for which Varian needed a sounding board; I could be of more use, he told me, rallying the troops under the enemy's nose. 'Thank you very much, sir,' I said, as I plodded off.

We had become semi-aquatic mammals, a kind of large and vicious water rat, living in and above the drainage ditches of the marsh, known to the men as 'wadis'. The platoons of B Company were dug into slit trenches on raised but chewed-up ground either side of one such wadi. These could be used to return to company headquarters or even to B Echelon, but to get into them you had to clamber thirty feet down a net. The forward trenches were for observation, sniping, mortar-bombing and so on during the night, which was the active part of the day; we had tried to dig sleeping areas where the men could rest, but they filled with water.

The four-square walls and solid roof of the Dormitory were memories of another age; battalion headquarters was now a mud-and-wattle palisade with the white crosses of temporary graves all round. The slit trenches were so shallow that they only protected you if you sat or lay; forward positions were connected by crawl trenches, though these were too tight to allow two men going different ways to pass on their bellies. The one on his way down, more recently under fire, was allowed to remain prone, leaving the other to risk standing. Casualties were inevitably high. Brian Pears and John Passmore were among the wounded and had been sent to Sicily to recover; their companies were both being led by their seconds in command.

It was true that every so often you could go down to B Echelon. Private Winter had got my camp bed set up in a dug-out inside the palisade and there was always an air-tight tin of Player's Navy Cut cigarettes and a bottle of whisky waiting. Though still within the range of German artillery, it felt safe; you could get clean clothes and read a book. Most men longed for it, but I was troubled by the noise of the nightingales when I tried to sleep and I found it impossible to deal with these two so different realities. I was glad when I was back in the wadis.

After weeks of this stalemate, I saw some of the best men begin to lose heart. The helplessness of our position was hard to bear. Even if we had been able to mount an attack and had successfully advanced, say, half a mile, the result would only have been more wadis and more digging but with longer lines of communication. Almost everyone had mutinous thoughts about the people in London who had dropped us into this throbbing, freezing hell.

It appeared that our commanders had decided we must

stay put in the beachhead until the Americans broke through at Cassino and came up to join us. Until this longed-for day, our job was to harass the Germans to the extent that they could not move any of their own troops back to Cassino. We had to occupy those who had us penned in. Or so Richard Varian guessed; there was no information actually given to us about Allied strategy.

Digging was a way of keeping warm in the forward trench at night. By day the best you could do was wriggle inside your clothes and hope for some friction; if you stood up or threw your arms about, you would be shot by a sniper. Bundles of clean socks came up each night from company headquarters, accompanied by rum. Distributing the liquor was a dangerous job, though, and one we had to rotate strictly; we lost Private Jones one evening, along with the rum ration.

One day I was in a forward trench with Bill Shenton and two others, trying to find a stable base for a cooker on which to brew tea at a hygienic distance from the shit-can, when Richard Varian crawled in.

'Sidwell's wounded,' he said. 'I was giving him his orders when he got hit in the groin by a shell splinter. He bled like a pig, poor man, but they think he'll pull through. How are you doing?'

'Never better,' I said. 'Poor Donald. What'll they do?'

'Get him to a hospital in Naples. He needs a proper surgeon. The trouble is the port's more dangerous than the beachhead now. They're bombing the hospital ships.'

'Would you like some tea, sir?' said Shenton.

'Yes, please, I've brought this.' Varian pulled out a hip flask. 'Help yourself.'

We sat waiting for the water to boil. At least there were British and American planes disputing the air above us; it made us feel that we were more than a diversion from the planned 'second front'. Shenton was a good tea-maker and we poured splashes of whisky into the boiling brown liquid when he dished it out. To feel something hot in your hands felt like a victory over the icy half-world.

'So,' said Varian. 'A Company no longer exists. Sidwell, Pears and Passmore are wounded. We're back to the real rump now.'

'That's no way to refer to Major Swann,' I said.

Shenton chuckled dutifully.

'Laugh all you can, Bill,' said Varian. 'These are the times that try men's souls.'

I looked at Varian's face in the drizzling rain – the almost black, unblinking eyes, the hair and dark moustache still neat for all the mud smears on his cheek and the drops of water falling from the rim of his helmet. How many men were there in the British army like him? People who could draw on what they knew, on what they'd seen – on what they'd read – to rise to the occasion . . . It was more than officer training, overseas postings and regular promotions. There was something about the way he accepted the circumstances of our rat existence in the marsh. He didn't rail against it; he submitted to the absurdity that fate, our commanders – or the mere sequence of events – had handed us. He made sure his servant ironed his battledress, that he had a new book to read, then crawled up to the front to reassure the men. He would never stop believing in his parents' house in Northumberland and the possibility of a normal world.

One morning I decided to go with Bill Shenton and find out exactly how near to us the enemy was dug in. About seventy yards was my guess.

This sounds suicidal, and perhaps it was. It was almost certainly wrong for an officer to take an NCO of Shenton's experience and value, but we were tired of rules. Nothing said I couldn't order a patrol. Taylor-West for one would have approved of the idea of keeping the enemy on his toes, and I had reached a stage where anything was preferable to the way we were living.

It was the time of day when by unspoken agreement things went quiet, when forward troops were replaced and went down the line to sleep. The idea was to find out exactly where the nearest Germans were, so we could both get word back to our artillery; but we were aware that there might be some action for us as we went along – some sport, as Bill Shenton put it.

What happened next is not clear in my mind. For many years I tried and failed to understand a sequence of events in which time seemed to collapse.

This is what I recall.

We dropped into the wadi and began to walk. The sides of the channel were naturally secured by the vertical roots of broken trees in the earth above; the passageway felt safe and permanent. We both had a knapsack of grenades. I'd got hold of an extra officer's pistol and given it to Bill.

The late winter rain was drifting over our heads as we moved along. After a couple of minutes, we could hear some attempts at tidying-up. A splatter of excrement fell just in front of us, hurled from its can in a trench. There was the sound of a song, softly voiced in German.

I had an idea that we could grab a Hun as he went about his ablutions and take him back to our line. Then we could find out what unit he was from and what other regiments were there. If we kept going for more than ten minutes down the wadi we would probably find ourselves at the headquarters of an enemy company. And if we waved a white flag, we could walk out of the war, like the German sleepers at the Dormitory. There'd be pea soup, sausage and pumpernickel, a lorry to a distant Stalag in the Fatherland, Red Cross socks and concert parties.

There was a young German, shirtless, trying to wash; he was plucking leaves from the tangled creeper of the wadi walls to scrape the mud from his chest.

'Don't do that, boy,' Mr Armitage was saying, smacking the side of his desk with a ruler held in his good hand.

There was the wet boom of enemy bombers going over our lines again towards the port.

'Give yourself up to the enemy?' said Sailor-Vest. 'You'll be shot at dawn if it's the last order I give!'

I closed my hand on the stock of my rifle. The trigger guard was icy on my skin. Rifles always hurt your fingers and if you wore gloves you couldn't feel the balance of the trigger when you squeezed.

'The *Anabasis* of Xenophon,' chimed Mr Liddell, 'has the exultant cry, "The sea, the sea", when after their long march the ten thousand set eyes on the Black Sea and can start to dream of their Greek homes.'

The rain was drifting up the wadi in gauzy, wavering curtains. It was hard to keep a sense of direction. It seemed to be coming from behind us as well. We were enfiladed by tumbling water.

Mary Miller said, 'I think this is the right thing to do, don't you, Robert?'

There was the single crack of a sniper.

'Don't do that, boy,' said Mr Armitage.

A ledge made by roots and fallen branches gave us a vantage point from which we could see six Germans hunched in a slit trench. I fished into my haversack for a grenade. Bill Shenton had the officer lined up through the sights of his rifle. I took the pin out of a grenade, waited, threw it, took the pin out of a second, waited, threw it, jumped down into the floor of the wadi and drove myself into a niche below the trench. A man put his face over the edge and Shenton shot him through the head.

We were in woods, in fields, I was running and

plunging through sodden undergrowth, brambles tearing at my legs. We were encircled by rain, a protective mist about us. I was coming to the brow of Pocock's field. I could still make out Shenton's tall figure, running at an even pace in front of me. I could hear machine-gun fire. It sounded like a Vickers, like a British gun. But we were behind German lines, I could tell by the shape of the church. I surged to the top of the hill and saw the mountains over Lake Königssee.

'Donald's dead!' I heard Varian shout. 'Sidwell's dead, he's dead!'

I wrote to Donald's mother and said he should have joined the navy after all.

What is a life? What is it worth? When a man dies you grow wise in a moment. You cover your shaming impotence, as if you understood. You give him his due, then carry on. But to your living men and to yourself you give a different care – as though you and the dead were not of the same kind. Their death raised an eyebrow; their life was a breath of weightless air. But yours, oh living souls, yours is heavy with meaning. As though you'd known in advance which life would be feathery and which one burdensome. But if you grant equal weight to a dead man's existence, you can't go on, you're finished too . . .

We were firing with rifles in the direction of the German line. We were lying flat in mud among the corpses of our men. Machine-gun bullets clanged from my helmet and I buried my face in slime but kept firing. I longed for the chance to bayonet, to feel flesh close – on the pig-sticker, steel on bone.

I was lying on my bed with the river under the window, I was waiting for Mary Miller to come and lie with me. To feel flesh close – membrane, skin.

If we hold out long enough, the Americans will come. If I take more bullets in my shoulder, in my chest, if we last another day the monastery will fall. If I can fire ten more rounds, one magazine, the men in Whitehall can tell each other that a plan, by luck and our blood, not their judgement, has worked enough that they can sleep tonight with easy minds.

My groin was pressed in Italian mud, the webbing of my belt and gaiters caked with it. The trigger was now hot with my fingering. We were in the mad minute when you get off thirty rounds. You fire so fast the enemy think you have machine guns. I emptied my haversack and tore the pins from the remaining grenades, one after the other, counting the intervals with a steady chime like the church clocks in Dresden, and launched them into the swirling rain.

I was lost. I was running again now in the wadi, towards our line, towards the enemy, I didn't know. I was fit with the strength of youth and the training of four years. I had taken the lessons of drill. 'You're like a string puppet, not a fucking soldier.' Not now. I was a runner who would never stop. I could run through bullets now, not even a shell could stop me.

'Follow me here, I'll look after you,' said my father.

I reached out my arms to him, but he slipped away from me, he slipped through my arms.

I'm running now, the rain is bullets, the drifting, wavering curtain of bullets, swirling down the drenched wadi, and I'm free to be a man, I'm free to be dead, I'm free to run and run.

A Week In December

AT ABOUT NINE o'clock, after the morning rush had subsided, Hassan al-Rashid took the Piccadilly Line to Manor House. He had received an address on a piece of paper sent from Salim, the head of his group, Muslim Youth Coalition, which was based in Bethnal Green. Salim believed the post was a safer way of contacting the members of the cell than e-mail. 'You might just as well write a letter to the local newspaper,' he told them. 'The spooks intercept all that stuff. Also, they can get your computer IP number from the websites you visit and they can track down your phone line and then your address, so if any of you have visited jihadist sites you'd better ditch your hard drive right now. If that means getting a new computer that stays completely clean, so be it. I have funds. I'll show you how to get rid of the old one.'

Following Salim's instructions, Hassan first downloaded some software called Drive+Nuke and selected

'Total' from the 'Level of Erasure' menu. He then took a hammer to the casing of his computer and extracted the hard disk. Rather to his surprise, it really was a disc, like a shiny CD and about the same size. In his father's shed he mixed fine-powdered iron oxide and aluminium, both of which he had taken from the lab at college, poured them through a funnel into an empty drinks can, then stuck a magnesium strip in the top. He took this, along with the hard drive, up on to the common at night, put the can on the disk, lit the magnesium strip and retreated. The drive was eliminated, as was the earth to a depth of more than a foot below it. Thermite, Salim told them, could reach a temperature of 4,000 degrees Fahrenheit. Hassan kicked some loose earth over the hole in the ground and made for home. Salim certainly didn't like to take chances.

His new machine, unfouled by Internet and e-mail history, remained in its box for a week. He couldn't find any legitimate use for it. Eventually, he thought he'd better download some songs, go on YourPlace or do a few of the things young people were supposed to do, so that if the police did come calling it would look normal. YourPlace was one of the most boring things he had ever seen. Pictures of millions of grinning *kafirs* whose lives were so empty it was fun for them to know that someone had 'jabbed' their photograph. Dear oh dear. It was almost a relief to know that the main practical use of the site was for sex; at least it had *some* function – for paedophiles to cruise, for teenage boys to rope in likely-looking girls for sex parties or for older *kafirs* to find 'fuck buddies'. Hassan visited the site daily, but left the room while his Internet record clocked up some plausible hours in this parody of a human world.

Today, he was going to meet for the first time the people with whom he was to wage jihad. The most famous group at this level of activity, boasting that it had precipitated coups in African states as well as fighting in Bosnia and Kuwait, was Hizb ut-Tahrir; but the alliance to which Hassan now belonged claimed to talk less than Hizb and to bomb more. It was called Husam Nar (which translated roughly, he knew from Arabic studies, as Burning Sword), though it rarely referred to itself by this or any other name; it was an organisation with no headquarters and no records. What it did have was money, and this, Salim told Hassan, came mostly from Saudi Arabia. This news was comforting to Hassan; to know that the money came from the country of Mecca and Medina reassured him in his new identity. Hassan's gradual progress from local mosque through youth organisations of gradually increasing extremism had been typical enough. The distinctive factor had been the single mentor, Salim. Most young men left behind their early guides in the course of their ascent, but Salim had been with Hassan from the beginning, like a wise uncle.

Today, he was going to meet for the first time the people with whom he was to wage jihad.

Having looked up the street name in the *A to Z*, Hassan memorised the route from the Tube station and ten minutes later found himself turning into a street with rusty Japanese cars along the kerb and a busy outdoor life – children, men and women of all ages talking in their front gardens, despite the cold, or smoking on the pavement. The house he was directed to looked as shabby as the rest, with one windowpane boarded up and thick grey net curtains on the ground floor. There were three bells by the front door, each with its own wire drilled through the jamb. Hassan pressed 'Ashaf', as instructed, and heard heavy footsteps on the uncarpeted hall. It was Salim.

'Come in, brother. You're the last to arrive.'

The others were gathered in the back room on the first floor. First, they knelt on the bare floorboards and prayed, facing Walthamstow.

One of them, Hassan noticed, seemed ill at ease. Although he bent low, he didn't seem to know the words of the prayers.

'All right, brothers,' said Salim. 'This house is ours for as long as we need it. We will all leave at different times, just as we arrived at twenty-minute intervals today. Don't speak to anyone in the street as you walk away, but don't be unfriendly. If someone asks you for a light or says hello, just smile vaguely. Do nothing anyone might remember. Now, I want you to introduce yourselves to one another and pick a *kafir* name that will be yours from now on. When you pick a name, it must be something easy to remember, something that's connected with where you come from. For instance, I'm from the East End so I'll call myself Alfie. It's an old cockney name.'

He nodded at a boy of about Hassan's age with the remains of acne showing through his sparse beard. He cleared his throat, but his voice caught nervously. 'My name is Akbar,' he said. 'As you can probably tell, I'm from Yorkshire.'

'Aye. 'appen.' This was said, in imitation of the Yorkshire accent, by the man who seemed not to know how to say his prayers properly; he was tall, about twenty-five, with a yellowish skin colour and a gold tooth. ''appen we'll call thee Seth, lad,' he said.

Salim looked at the youth. 'Is that all right? Seth?'

The boy nodded, though he didn't look happy about it.

'Where are you from?' Hassan asked the man with the gold tooth.

'My name is Ravi. I'm from Leicester.' He looked at them challengingly.

'That doesn't sound like a Muslim name,' said Hassan.

'I was born a Hindu. I converted,' said Ravi. 'Do you have a problem with that?'

Hassan shook his head. It did seem odd to him that someone not born Muslim should be engaged on jihad, but he couldn't explain why. 'No,' he said. 'No problem.'

'I don't suppose you can think of anyone famous from Leicester, can you?' said Ravi.

'Gary,' said Hassan.

'Who's Gary then?'

'A footballer,' said Hassan. 'Their most famous ever player.'

'Gary's good,' said Salim. 'Now you.' He nodded at Hassan.

'My name is Hassan,' he said. 'And I'm from–'

'Och aye,' said Gary, né Ravi. 'I think we all know where ye're frae, MacTavish.'

'There's a name that I was called once and it really angered me,' said Hassan. 'Someone called me "Jock". If I'm going to die, I'd like to take that name down with me.'

Salim nodded. 'All right. We'll call you Jock.'

The last of the five said, 'My name's Hanif and I'm from Watford.' He was bald and thickset, unlike the others, all of whom looked hungry. 'I bet you can't name a footballer from Watford.'

'Bet I could,' said Hassan, 'but why don't we call you Elton?'

'Elton?'

'Elton. He's the chairman. Or he was.'

'It's good,' said Salim.

'You seem to know a lot,' said Elton.

'He's the brains,' said Salim. 'He's our college boy.'

Gary the Gold Tooth Hindu, thought Hassan. Seth the Shy One. And Bald Elton. It was easy enough. What would be harder was to remember to call Salim 'Alfie' from now on.

Hassan had a sudden and terrible desire to laugh – at the thought of roly-poly Elton John with his diamanté glasses and his boyfriend and his platform heels having unwittingly given his name to a solemn would-be terrorist . . . Salim had occasionally had cause to rebuke him for his descent into laughter: it showed spiritual immaturity, he said. Hassan did believe in purity and truth with all his might; but he had been brought up in a godless country where television and newspapers mocked the social structures night and day . . .

'And we'll call this place "the pub",' Salim was saying. 'So if you hear someone say, "I'm meeting Alfie down the pub" it couldn't sound more normal, more everyday *kafir*.'

'When do we get our instructions then?' asked Seth.

Salim coughed and walked round the unfurnished room. 'In a couple of days. For security reasons, it's best if you don't know in advance.'

'Why?' said Gary. 'It's not as if we're going to –'

'For heaven's sake, didn't you learn anything in Pakistan?' Hassan hadn't seen Salim impose himself like this before. 'It's rudimentary. All knowledge is potentially a leak. You are told only what you need to know and not one thing more. The only reason you're meeting together today is that you'll need to recognise one another. I also think it's a good idea to form a bond. But this is as far as it goes. I don't even know the real name of my superior. I meet him in different places – cafés, parks, even in a pub one time. I just know him as Steve.'

'And what are we going to do on the day?' said Elton.

'We are going to wage jihad. Each of you has a task. Jock is doing the shopping. Seth and Elton will assemble the ingredients. Gary will help me plan the route and the timing. We'll all plant the bombs. Today is Monday. We need Jock to have brought everything here by Thursday morning so that Seth and Elton can put it all together.'

'Do we know where we're going?' said Gary.

'Yes. I've already been there and had a good look. But I won't be telling you until we meet on Friday.'

'What time on Friday?' said Hassan.

'I'll let you know the day before. Why?'

'It's just . . .' Hassan stopped. 'It's difficult to explain. My father is . . . is . . .' He felt his throat constrict. He was frightened of Salim's anger.

'What is it?' said Salim.

'My father is going to Buckingham Palace to get the OBE,' said Hassan. 'And my mother and I have to go with him.'

There was silence in the little upstairs room. Hassan sensed that the others were not sure whether they should laugh or be indignant. They looked to Salim for a lead.

He spoke very quietly. 'The work of the Prophet will take place at its appointed time. And you will be there. I shall give you the exact timings on Thursday, not a moment before.'

Hassan nodded. He quickly considered the various

excuses he could offer to his parents. 'Sickness' wouldn't work: his father would compel him to come, however ill he claimed to be. He would simply have to go out the night before to Pudding Mill Lane and not return. He would later have to claim a loss of memory, an accident with a car or something. His parents would be so pleased that he was safe that they'd forget their disappointment at his absence from the palace.

'How will you be in touch? Still post?' said Elton.

'Have you heard of steganography?' said Salim.

Elton shook his head.

'It's a way of embedding text in a computer file so that it can't be seen unless you have the right kit for decoding it. I'm going to give you an Internet link and I need you to check it daily. As you know I've preferred the post till now, but it could be that in the last forty-eight hours things will move too fast for the Royal Mail. So we need a fallback. There's a *kafir* porn site called babesdelight.co.uk. It's not hard filth like most of them. It's just naked girls, that's all, the kind of thing they sell in their most famous high-street family stationer. You get a choice of lots of pictures – sets of pictures in fact. There's a box called "Search for your girl" and in that you type "Olya". She's some Russian hooker. Anyway, the main picture of her, the big money shot, is the tenth, the last on the page. Click and open it up big. Embedded in that, in a particularly intimate place, will be any last-minute instructions. You'll need to check it hourly from Wednesday at noon. It's the last place the spooks would expect people like us to be communicating.'

'How do we get to read the hidden message?' said Seth.

'You can download the tools. Dead simple. The program you want – and you must remember this – is called Stegwriter. You need the Gamma version 16. Got that? Some of the instructions for encoding are in German, but that's OK. I can handle that. Of course it's more complicated using an image already on the Web rather than one from my own photo collection, but I have a great little geek to help me. Anyway, decoding is easy for you guys. You download your program. What's it called again? Seth?'

'Stegwriter, Gamma version 16.'

'Good man. Then basically, you follow the prompts. Open the photo of the girl on – what's the site, Elton?'

'Babesdelight.co.uk.' Elton didn't relish saying the words.

'Right. Then open up Stegwriter. Click on File manager and then Decrypt. Follow the prompts. My problem was that in order to hide data of any size I had to find a file that was proportionate. Eventually I found a 650-kilobyte WAV file would carry a five-byte text file. Stegwriter has the whole kit.'

Seth coughed. 'Is it right to be looking at these pictures? I know that in the name of the Prophet . . .'

Salim looked at Seth sorrowfully. 'There is nothing in life that is moral or immoral, there is only the command of God. If Allah has forbidden something, then it is wrong.

I am not aware that he has forbidden us to look at women. In fact, there is an early scriptural source in which devout men look at the reflection of a naked woman as she is preparing to bathe. Another authority tells us a man may inspect his wife before marrying her, to make sure she is without blemish that might harm their children.'

'But I don't intend to marry Olya,' said Elton.

'But you can still look. Some scholars of Arabic have argued that the word means very much more than "look" in English.'

'I think I'd feel uneasy.'

'Islam does not recognise "feeling uneasy", it only cares about what God has commanded. You're talking like a Christian, some ridiculous Catholic. In any event, Seth, the important issue is not whether your eyes have rested for a moment on a naked woman, but whether you can play your part in ushering in the new caliphate.'

When it was his turn to leave the house and walk back to the Tube station, Hassan also felt 'uneasy'. There were a large number of Muslim girls at his college and when some of them took to wearing the hijab, he supported them, as did the other serious male students. What he didn't dare admit was that he found the black covering attractive, particularly with girls he had previously seen in Western clothes. Rania, for instance, used to wear grey skirts and leather boots, so her dress was modest, revealing only her knees, shiny beneath navy blue tights, when she sat down in the lecture hall. On her upper half she wore a white blouse, buttoned high, and a cardigan or jacket. There was nothing to distress her parents in all this. But in her eyes . . . She applied a thin line of black and a trace of mascara in the Ladies after she'd arrived in the morning, and her lashes were long. The grey skirt, though knee-length, did cling to her hips, and if Hassan happened to be watching when she innocently crossed her legs, he glimpsed for a moment the deep blue thighs and the darkness beyond. He had the contours of Rania's body so deeply etched in his mind that when she took to wearing the hijab it wasn't, to begin with, any hardship for him. He saw through it. The clean white bra and underpants that he could picture beneath, the thighs presumably still in the same navy blue nylon, the curve of the hips and the smallish, firm breasts . . . Now the eyes had no trace of liner or mascara, but when the long lashes were lowered over the dark brown iris there was still a message of invitation.

The scriptural reference to 'looking' was one that had been popular among his friends, as it seemed to excuse so much. One of them pointed out to Hassan a passage from a Koranic scholar that read: 'The dual nature of what is shown and what is concealed is fundamental to the understanding of God; and this double aspect is explicitly linked in at least one place to sexuality, where the female genitals are identified with the concealed aspect of the divine. There are no Islamic monks. The Prophet had many wives, and we are urged to copulate and procreate.

Many scholars have seen orgasm as a foretaste of paradise, where the sensation will not be brief, but eternal.'

One of the boys at college, who had a large collection of top-shelf magazines, told Hassan it was fine if the girls in the pictures were *kafirs*. Hassan thought this was making a virtue of necessity, since Muslim women simply didn't pose nude. His own aesthetic taste was always for dark-haired women of his own background; leaving aside his sinful thoughts about Rania's body, he simply liked the elegance and colouring of these women, their femininity.

It was a torment that seldom let up. At the age of nineteen, before he became religious, he had had a *kafir* girlfriend, a white Londoner called Dawn who was in the same year at college. It seemed to be just his luck that he had found the only sexually reticent *kafir* in London. Parts of the West End were no-go zones on Friday and Saturday nights with drunken girls in tiny skirts showing their breasts to passers-by before they threw up in the gutter. Friends of his at college told awed tales of the licentiousness of ever-willing *kafir* girls. But Dawn, for some reason she couldn't properly explain, allowed Hassan only limited access. He could put his hands beneath her clothes and touch her between the legs, but that was all. She refused to reciprocate. It was only when he (to his self-admitted shame) suggested to her that her reluctance was due to some atavistic racial prejudice that she tearfully relented. It was in a flat she shared with three other girls in Stamford Hill, with the thump of noisy dance music coming from the lounge. Dawn was rigid with resistance, then with cold, in her unheated bedroom as she lay naked at last beneath the duvet. Hassan was scared they might be interrupted by one of the flatmates, all of whom, this being a Friday night, were stupefied with drink. It wasn't at all how he had hoped it might be. Dawn insisted on turning out the bedside lamp, depriving him of the stimulus of sight. When he lay down on top of her, she seemed to shudder a little; he thought perhaps she was crying. He told her that they didn't have to go ahead, but she replied that now they had got this far he might as well finish it off. Hassan felt the pent desires of seven years since puberty compressing to a hard explosive point. Then as Dawn's cold hands stroked his back without enthusiasm, the moment seemed to pass him by. After twenty minutes or more of fumbling and apology and desperate measures, he managed something – a sort of end point without any preceding sensation. He was too ashamed of himself to see her again.

A few weeks later, he found his attention increasingly focussing on a tall and amusing Iranian called Shahla Hajiani, and it seemed to him that his interest was reciprocated. But by then he'd found religion, or a political version of it. When, after a student party, Shahla placed a modest but flirtatious hand on his arm, he explained to her that he must lead a pure life. She looked at him with sad eyes, in which there was still laughter, but also a little hurt and bafflement. 'I'll be your friend, then,' she said. 'If that's allowed?'

'Of course it is.'

And she had been a good friend, too, he had to admit. Shahla's father was a Westernised Tehran businessman who had left the country with the fall of the Shah; her mother was English, of part Jewish descent. Shahla, though nominally Muslim, didn't understand or approve of Hassan's mosque life; but she had been solicitous and kind at college, generous with her time and company, swinging through the canteen on her long legs, shoulder bag flying, to settle down beside him over lunch. Sometimes Hassan thought he could still see a glimmer of hope, or lust, or something, in her deep brown eyes. Mostly, she asked him innocent questions or told him what play or film she'd been to see and gave an animated account of it.

Thinking of the eternal fires that waited for the unbeliever, particularly an apostate like Shahla, Hassan felt he should ignore her. Yet her friendliness was so unassuming that he found himself, against his better judgement, absorbed by what she said.

. . .

HASSAN LEFT HIS parents at the palace, his father stunned, his mother pink with fussy pride, and walked up over the grass to Green Park Tube station on the Piccadilly Line.

At last, he thought, I am back in real life, back with things that matter. In the train, he took off his tie and stuffed it in his pocket. He was due at 'the pub' at 12.40, having asked Salim if he could be the last to arrive. The timing would be tight, but such was his elation that he wasn't worried. It was God's work, God's will.

He'd read accounts of Islamist groups in the *kafir* press and he'd read fine writing about what went on in the heads of 'terrorists'; he'd seen a 'drama-documentary' in the cinema about the planes that crashed into the Towers. What no one talked about, no one seemed to understand, was the joy – the pure exhilaration of belief!

People like himself were portrayed as madmen, mumbling, but as the Tube train rattled up to Manor House, he had never felt more lucid. It was all, as Ali had pointed out to them in Bradford, so simple. Life did not need string theory, eleven dimensions and a battering of the head against the inherent contradictions of human consciousness. All it required was to follow a simple revealed truth. There it was, on the bookshelf for £6.99. For all time. What was more amazing, the glorious purity of the truth or the boneheaded refusal of people to accept the gift that had been given them?

Hassan went down the lazy street with its outdoor life for what he thought would be the last time, and rang the bell marked 'Ashaf'. Salim let him in. Upstairs were Gary the Gold Tooth Hindu, Seth the Shy One and Bald Elton.

There were four rucksacks sitting in the middle of the bare wooden floor.

In the corner, with his back to them, looking over the

scrap of garden was someone Hassan hadn't seen before. The man turned round.

'This is Steve from Husam Nar,' said Salim. 'Steve, this is Jock.'

Steve was a short, tubby man of African appearance, about thirty years old. 'In these bags,' he said, 'are bomb components. We've used hydrogen peroxide injected into drinks bottles. This is a development of what was due to be used on those aircraft, where you need only a fairly small explosion to bring the plane down. We needed more bang, so each of you is carrying twenty-five drinks bottles. The detonators are in disposable cameras. The battery contents have been replaced by HMTD, or to give it the proper name, hexamethylene triperoxide diamine. This works as the primary explosive, or primer. It's unstable enough to go off easily, but stable enough to transport. Next to it in the battery casing is a small light bulb. When the camera is turned on, the charge to the light bulb is enough to detonate the HMTD which in turn sets off the main explosive. All clear?'

They all nodded. Steve had a thick East African accent, but his words were easy enough to follow.

'Listen carefully. You each go separately to the target. There are no trial runs. At the target you reassemble. You choose exactly where in a minute. One of you will carry all the detonators because we can't risk travelling on the train with the detonators in the same bag as the explosive.

They're in this fourth bag here. Once you're at your assembly point at the target, the detonators are given out and the man who brought them is given his share of explosive by the other three. You've chosen?'

'Yes,' said Salim. 'Jock will take the detonators.'

'OK,' said Steve. 'The timing is that you meet at 11 p.m. tomorrow. You travel alone. You make your own travel plan. If you're on the same train and happen to see one another, ignore it. The target is fifteen minutes' walk from a busy railway station so there's no problem about getting there. You need to leave plenty of time, but not too much. Hanging around can be dangerous. Give yourself half an hour leeway but no more.'

The atmosphere in the room had become tense. Hassan no longer felt elated. Something about the charmless, practical way that Steve drove onwards made him feel, for the first time, extremely frightened.

From inside his coat pocket, Steve took out a folded piece of paper. When he opened it out fully, it was the size of a lecturer's flip chart. He laid it flat on the table.

'This,' he said, 'is Glendale Hospital. The local railway station is fifteen minutes this way. The map is not to scale because you need to see the layout of the different units in detail. The first three will be detonating here, here and here. The greatest density of patients is in this building here. It's possible that the first blast will be such that it will detonate the second without you needing to use the camera. Because of the long corridor that joins this outbuilding with the main hospital, the blast should be funnelled through into the main building, which is where the fourth and largest bomb will be placed. The outbuildings form a specialised psychiatric unit, but the main building is a general hospital, and the wing attached here, where the fourth blast will be, has "longterm" units on the first floor – people who are dying, basically – and then the maternity unit on the floor above. Our experts chose this site because of its particular vulnerability. The psychiatric clinic has quite low security, only two porters on the main gate, just here, and simple signing-in at a desk inside. But my ballistics man in Pakistan told me that this joining corridor, which is really there for catering trolleys and things, this bit here, will magnify and funnel the blast and so help with the bomb in the main building. We don't need to go into all those details now. What we do need is for each of you to have a very clear picture in his head of this layout and of where your rucksack is going to be put down. So come and have a close look. Once you've got the overall plan clear I'll show you photographs of the interiors.'

The four men gathered round beneath the eye of Steve and Salim.

Hassan inspected the red-felt outlines of Collingwood, Beardsley, Arkell . . . He tried to be businesslike and cool, but a question kept shaping itself in his mouth. He was glad it wasn't him but quiet Yorkshire Seth who finally spoke.

'So . . . Are you saying we're attacking a hospital?'

'Yes.'

'I . . . I . . .'

Seth seemed unable to continue.

None of the others spoke. Perhaps, Hassan thought, by not acknowledging that there might be an issue, Steve and Salim were hoping to kill any hesitation at birth. They merely gazed at Seth.

Eventually, Steve spoke. 'It's an ideal target. It ticks all three boxes. News impact. Density of population. And third, though this is less important, scarcity of Muslim victims. You may or may not know that the Muslim population is under-represented in hospitals. There are no alcohol-related illnesses, fewer obese people with diabetes and so on. The figures are even better in psychiatric care. As far as density of people is concerned, it's not as good as the Tube, but security on the Underground is now so tight that it's become impossible. For news impact a hospital is even better than the transport system. Personally, I don't feel that Muslim presence or absence is of great concern considering that any believer who dies will be assured of his place in paradise. But there were some people who felt uneasy about the Edgware Road Tube bomb going off in such an Arab area, where so many passers-by were likely to be Muslim. All clear?'

'Yes,' said Seth. 'But . . . You know . . .'

'No, I don't.'

'For fuck's sake,' said Gary, the ex-Hindu. 'If we're trying to build a just world by undermining what is unjust, what difference does it make if someone's having their appendix out?'

'I know, but–'

'Having a sprained ankle doesn't make them any less a part of the *Jahiliyya*.'

'I just . . . No, you're right.'

'You're not thinking some *kafir* shit about "fair play" or something, because–'

'No, no, stop it. I understand. Stop it. I'm sorry I mentioned it.'

When the silence had been left for about twenty seconds, Steve said, 'All right. Four bombs. You number from one to four. One, two, three, four.' He prodded them each in the chest with a number. 'Now we'll look at the photographs of the interior. Memorise them.'

. . .

ONCE UP ON Waterloo Bridge, Hassan began to walk south. Halfway across the river, he came to a halt with a strange, panicky feeling: there was no sign of Waterloo station on the other side. He stopped and tried to regain his bearings. Behind him, he remembered a huge building with a courtyard. He thought it was Somerset House. Ahead, he could see a cluster of equally large buildings in a brutal modernist style, but he didn't know what they were. Theatres, galleries? He looked, in vain, for the arched roof of a railway station. It wasn't there.

He didn't know whether to go on or turn back; he had no way of orientating himself. Then he remembered how this had happened to him once before, when the GPO Tower appeared to be in the wrong place. His mother had told him it was because he had been too long without food and his blood-sugar levels had crashed; this led to mental confusion and could be dangerous, Nasim had read, because he might faint and his brain could be damaged by lack of oxygen. She insisted that he see a doctor, who told him it was called 'hypoglycaemia' and could be cured at once by a simple bar of chocolate. It was true he'd eaten nothing today since a piece of toast with his parents at about nine – more than twelve hours ago. But how could you lose an international mainline station, however low your blood sugar? How could it just disappear?

Hassan found sweat on his upper lip despite the increasing cold of the night. His hands were both shaking now, though whether from fear or from hypoglycaemia he didn't know. Then he had an idea. His rucksack had a compass sewn into the top flap; it was part of the kit. He knelt down on the pavement and fumblingly undid it. If it showed north behind him and south ahead, across the bridge, then surely all he needed to do was carry on.

When he had finally obtained a reading, it told him he was heading south-east. Yet surely the Thames ran west–east, so he could only be going north or south across it. The compass had simply made things worse.

Someone was coming towards him on the footpath of the bridge and Hassan decided to ask him the way. But as he came closer, it was clear that the man was plugged into loud music from his earpiece and couldn't be distracted. A woman was crossing the other way, but she was talking into a mobile phone and didn't see Hassan when he waved at her.

Above the almost freezing Thames, Hassan stood, trying to persuade a passing Londoner – anyone – to engage with him.

A strange memory came to him in his light-headedness. Waterloo station was not at the foot of Waterloo Bridge; perplexingly, it was at the foot of Westminster Bridge. No. That was irrational, impossible. And anyway, when he looked upstream there was a rattling railway bridge – Hungerford, was it – not the stately Westminster. Where now was Westminster Bridge? Had that gone too? Or maybe the Thames took a sudden turn and ran north–south at this point, in which case he should be going . . . East?

Oh God, he thought, oh God. I mustn't lose it now. He muttered a prayer, then turned back for human help.

Five people he tried to stop on the bridge; five times he moved forward and tried to intercept these passing strangers, and five times he found them wrapped up in private music or talking into hands-free microphones concealed in their coats.

They were talking to the air. All were listening to

voices, talking back, but there were no people. His was the only real voice on the bridge, but the only one to whom no one would listen.

He couldn't give up now. He couldn't stop. What he had to do was somehow to make the world hear – not the profane nonsense of rap and rock, not the garbage of *kafir* phone calls, but the truth and beauty of another voice: the words of the unseen God, spoken to the Prophet almost 1,400 years ago. Those were the words that must reverberate in the ears of the people on the bridge, and in the ears of all the world.

At that moment a bicycle with no lights on shot past him along the pavement, making him leap to one side.

Hassan stood back against the parapet of the bridge, with his heart hammering his ribs in a huge lumping rhythm. Shit. He had thought for a second he was going to die.

His body wouldn't return to normal; he couldn't get a rhythm back. It was hard to breathe.

Then he leaned forward on the stone parapet and put his head between his hands. Where was it? Where was the voice, the voice of God that the Prophet had heard in the desert? This was the voice of the truth, the world's salvation. This was what he must die for. What he must kill for. For that disembodied voice only and not for any other, he must go to the station, go to the hospital and kill.

It was all so fantastically, so risibly, improbable.

Hassan hoisted himself onto the parapet so he could

see down into the icy darkness of the river below, the oily surface sweating black.

He thought of his mother Nasim's earnest face, leaning over his bed and of his father's dear worried eyes with those little specks of pigment under them.

His heart was still pounding from where the unlit bicyclist had brought him face to face with reality.

And as he moaned like a wolf in a trap, a strange thing began to happen in his mind. He found that his pumping heart began to slow, and as it brought him back from the edge of death, his moaning began to soften; and in the bellows of his chest it mutated slowly into something deep, and uncontrolled and wholly unexpected that felt like – that in fact turned out to be – laughter.

Hassan knelt on all fours and laughed; then he rolled on to his side and hunched up in a ball to try to bring relief to his airless lungs.

When he could stand again and could breathe unimpeded, he slowly unhitched his rucksack and lowered it on to the paving stone. He thought carefully before the next movement. With deliberation, unhurried, he hoisted the bag on to the parapet.

He stood back and looked both ways to be sure that no one was watching. Then, with both hands, he gave the rucksack an unequivocal shove. A moment later, he heard it splash into the Thames and pictured it as it sank into the dark, forgiving water. No explosion disturbed the current.

Then he turned back, pulled his own mobile phone from his pocket and scrolled down the stored names till he found the one he wanted. 'Hello?' 'Hello?' Don't say there was no bloody signal. 'Hello? Is that Shahla? Can you hear me? OK. Great. Look. I'm sorry to ring so late . . . I was wondering if . . . I was wondering if I could possibly come round. What? Yes. Now. I'm really sorry, I wouldn't ask unless . . . You are kind. I really appreciate it. No, no don't go to any trouble. OK. See you in a bit.'

He had £100 emergency money from Husam Nar and £40 of his own, so a taxi fare was not a problem. He crossed the river and hailed a black cab at the roundabout.

Hassan sat back and sighed. Now that the laughter had passed, he felt shaken and empty. He had betrayed a cause and left three men exposed to danger. There was in practical terms nothing they could do without the fuses and the primer; presumably when they had waited long enough, they would simply ditch their rucksacks, separate and go home. He himself would be in some difficulties with MYC and Husam Nar; he would have to give solemn undertakings of secrecy to Salim. Two things worked in his favour, however. Many young men went through periods of activism and training without ever engaging in positive action; the organisations were practised in dealing with them: they knew how to retain their interest for possible future use or how to debrief, deactivate and disown them. The second thing was that the system of cut-outs was so well arranged that he knew nothing of value: no names or addresses or personal details of any kind that could be passed on. The 'pub' would be re-let at once to an immigrant family. As for 'Salim', he didn't even know if that was his real name, any more than 'Alfie' or 'Grey_Rider'.

The taxi went down Albert Embankment, and Hassan looked out at the lights along the Thames. He was not a soldier, he was not a jihadi or a terrorist or whatever term people might use. But was he still a believer? Had he failed even in that? It was too soon to say. His thoughts were too turbulent for him to be able to take stock of what he now thought. But something had happened on that bridge. Something more than the shock of almost being knocked down by a speeding cyclist . . . Something profound and real at that moment had changed in him, had shifted on its axis; and it was never going back.

Down Wandsworth Road the taxi went rapidly through a sequence of green lights, making Hassan worry that Shahla wouldn't have time to prepare herself; she had sounded confused by sleep when she answered the phone. Now they were outside her house, his taxi the only noise, ticking and throbbing in the narrow street. He paid the driver and watched him disappear before touching Shahla's bell. He heard her on the stairs, coming down to the front door, then saw the anxiety in her face under the 60-watt hall bulb in its paper lantern shade.

He was shaking – with cold, he thought – as he sat down in her living room. Shahla lit the gas fire, then went to the kitchen and returned with two cups of tea. He was in the armchair, and she sat on the edge of the coffee table so that her knees, at the end of those long thighs, were against his.

She was wearing pyjama bottoms, a college sweatshirt and what Hassan was fairly sure were skiing socks. Her long, dark hair was tousled from her bed and she smelled slightly of toothpaste as she leaned forward and said, 'So what's all this about, Hass?'

He smiled sheepishly. 'I'm not sure I know where to begin.'

'Try.'

'I think I may have been . . . Misled.'

'Go on.'

'It's so kind of you to let me come round like this and –'

'Don't worry about all that now. Just tell me. Misled. How?'

Hassan breathed in tightly. 'It's very difficult in life to know what's valuable, what's lasting. Even to know what's real.'

Shahla nodded. A slight smile broke though her solicitous expression, reminding Hassan of how much more she always seemed to know than he did.

Slowly, Hassan put together a few words that seemed to come close to what he meant. 'Maybe I was not as lonely as I thought.'

© Muir Vidler

SEBASTIAN FAULKS was born in Berkshire in 1953. His father was a solicitor who had interrupted his training in 1939 to enlist with the Duke of Wellington's, a Yorkshire-based infantry regiment, while his grandfather had served in the Artists Rifles in the First World War.

Sebastian worked briefly as a teacher before becoming a journalist, joining first the *Daily Telegraph* and then the *Independent*, where he was Literary Editor at its launch in 1986. He left journalism to write full time in 1991 and the success of his fourth novel *Birdsong* (1993) meant that he never returned to newspapers.

He is now the author of thirteen novels and three works of non-fiction. He lives in west London with his wife, who is a bookseller, and two of their three children (the eldest, William, works as a football reporter in Spain). He was elected a Fellow of the Royal Society of Literature in 1993 and appointed CBE for services to literature in 2002. He is a member of the Authors XI cricket team and the Boffins CC, and plays tennis in the West Middlesex leagues for his local club, Campden Hill.

RECOMMENDED BOOKS BY SEBASTIAN FAULKS:

Charlotte Gray
Engleby
Human Traces

VINTAGE MINIS

The Vintage Minis bring you some of the world's greatest writers on the experiences that make us human. These stylish, entertaining little books explore the whole spectrum of life – from birth to death, and everything in between. Which means there's something here for everyone, whatever your story.

Desire	Haruki Murakami
Love	Jeanette Winterson
Marriage	Jane Austen
Babies	Anne Enright
Language	Xiaolu Guo
Motherhood	Helen Simpson
Fatherhood	Karl Ove Knausgaard
Summer	Laurie Lee
Jealousy	Marcel Proust
Sisters	Louisa May Alcott
Home	Salman Rushdie
Race	Toni Morrison
Liberty	Virginia Woolf
Swimming	Roger Deakin
Friendship	Rose Tremain
Work	Joseph Heller
Money	Yuval Noah Harari
Austerity	Yanis Varoufakis
Injustice	Richard Wright
War	Sebastian Faulks
Depression	William Styron
Drinking	John Cheever

Eating	Nigella Lawson
Rave	Irvine Welsh
Psychedelics	Aldous Huxley
Calm	Tim Parks
Dreams	Sigmund Freud
Ghosts	M. R. James
Freedom	Margaret Atwood
Death	Julian Barnes